The Hajj

Rashid Begg
The Hajj

© 2013 Rashid Begg
Layout, cover design, printing and publication: BoD – Books on Demand, Germany
ISBN: 978-3-7322-2690-0

Inhalt

Chapter 1: The Beginning	7
Chapter 2: Memoirs of the Sacred	15
Chapter 3: The Sufi	24
Chapter 4: The Hijra Reversed	32
Chapter 5: The Black Stone	42
Chapter 6: The Cave	51
Chapter 7: The Heifer	60
Chapter 8: The Narratives of Imam Arabi	68
Chapter 9: The Kiswah	76
Chapter 10: The Memory of Sheikh Mahmood Vaybier	78
Chapter 11: The Teachings of the Urdu Cleric	88
Chapter 12: The Plains of Mount Araf at	95
Chapter 13: Al-Mash'aril-Haraam	104
Chapter 14: Mina and the Visions of 911	111
Chapter 15: Farewell to the Sacred	118

Chapter 1: The Beginning

> *"Bismillah-hir-rahman-nir-raheem"*
> *[With the name of Allah, the Beneficent, the Merciful]*

It has been almost a decade now since this journey started. The world then was very different from the world I live in now. I, Kimal Baig, am still surrounded by friends and family of the old world even though my new world includes many who are willing to listen, often with reserve, to the ideas and rationalizations of my new reality.

But let me start at the beginning. It all started in the year of the Lord 2000 in the harbour city of Port Elizabeth, South Africa. Given the social history of the locals, race permeated every institution of the environment. Black people lived then, as they still do today, in the townships created by the apartheid engineers of the pre-Mandela era. Coloured people were firmly entrenched in their designated townships and white people in neighbourhoods that distinctly spoke of upward social mobility. Social stratification was clearly structured along racial lines even though the rhetoric of apartheid's demise was ubiquitously evident in the discourses of would-be believers.

I must state at this juncture that this story is not about race, but about a religious journey: to the sacred and the profane. However, to ignore the primary marker in my world, race, would be an injustice to those both in the townships and the affluent ones in the comfort of suburbia. Separate racial development had the latent effect of causing those of colour to commune together. And in this oppressive world religion came to offer the much sought after opium to lull the harsh indignities and insults that overt racism imposed. My reality was Coloured and Muslim. More precisely, a Deobandi version of Islam that had made its way from South Asia to the southern parts of South Africa at the beginning of the 1860s and had found roots in this region through the Madressa institutions. My skin colour determined my identity. There are many varieties of mixed heritage that fall under the constructed category 'Coloured'. Mine is a blend of South Asian-German-Kurdish-Turkish-South East Asian.

Given my Deobandi leanings, my garb, my attitude, all of my being was directed in a very specific way. Sporting a rather large unkempt beard rustled with too many strands of grey hairs there was no disputing my religious affiliation. These facial markers that supported the image of an Islamic Fundamentalist, so I was told, fitted well with the many long thaubs (caftans) that we Deobandis wear. Here in South Africa Deobandis are often mistaken for Tablighi followers. The lines are blurry. This is not surprising given the many similar religious rituals we follow. Be that as it may, there was no mistaking who I was.

My partner in life, the innocent 20 year old Shireen, was, judged by any lens, beautiful and demure. I sometimes wonder at my luck but am told that I should thank Allah for his mercy. At the ripe old age of forty, I was inclined to go with this line of rationalization.

Even though both Shireen and I were staunch Muslims we had to this point never entertained the idea of embarking on the holy pilgrimage to Mecca (Hajj). We were too young. The Hajj was a passport to janna (heaven) since all were said to be forgiven after this last sacred pillar of Islam was performed, and any thinking person would attest that you do this at an advanced age since the time left for sin would be greatly diminished then. At forty I counted on at least a couple of decades before applying for that guaranteed passport to heaven. Besides, I thought, Shireen was only twenty and definitely too young to embark on a lifetime of commitment to all that is good.

Then there was also the baby, Shameer, just two months old to consider. We considered Shameer to be literally a gift from Allah as Shireen had contracted German measles during the first trimester of her pregnancy. After visiting a number of specialists it was confirmed that the baby's chance of being born unaffected was less than five percent. Our last resort was to get the Sheikh's blessing for an abortion. In our community the word abortion is not mentioned out of respect for elders who find the word anathema to the religion. In our case there was to be no dispute about the matter. The Sheikh needed to be consulted. And not any Sheikh, it had to be the grand Mufti of Cape Town. Hurriedly we packed our bags for our trip to the mother city some eight hundred kilometers from our coastal city of Port Elizabeth.

The Sheikh was young, maybe thirty-two. It was hard for him to stay focused as his eyes kept returning to Shireen. It was as if I was not present. The youth of this cleric did not match the abundance of wisdom that he poured forth. Part of his wisdom infused his fatwa: Shireen was to abort the baby.

Tears silently ran down Shireen's cheeks as we left the living room of the learned Sheikh. Turning to Shireen as soon as we were out of the Sheikh's gaze, I asked her how she felt. "I will keep the baby no matter what Allah has in store for me," was her certain response. I knew then that this was to be our way forward. With both the medical specialist and the Muslim clerics pushing for termination of the pregnancy, all we had left was Shireen's faith. Since my own faith waned in comparison to Shireen's, I was happy to ride on hers.

Not a day would pass that I would not witness Shireen in tears on the prayer mat in her bedroom. On occasion I enquired why she was crying so much. Her response was quite unexpected, "In gratitude to Allah for giving me this child".

At a few days past term Shireen took seriously ill. The doctor grew quite pale when he examined her, and in a nervous voice said, "The fetal heart rate is above two hundred and fifty, we have to take it out now". The caesarian section was done immediately. Out came Shameer with a distinct odour that still permeates my nostrils. There was nothing wrong with him as far as we or the doctors could tell. Nothing of the high levels of immunoglobulins or the statistical probabilities spoken of showed any sign of truth.

Nervously we waited for the pre-birth medical predictions to show over the next few months. Shameer was perfectly normal.

More than normal, Shireen confidently reported that he was strong and manly. "Just look at the fine hairs on his back," she would say with a wry smile on her face.

In return for His favour we decided to go on the holy pilgrimage to Mecca. Shameer was to remain behind in the care of Shireen's mother in Cape Town. My immediate concern was for Shireen's emotional condition leaving Shameer in someone else's care so soon after the fragile pregnancy. Shireen had no concern.

She was happy to serve the God who gave her the miracle of birth whilst defying the medical odds so heavily stacked against her. I was not immediately convinced – perhaps my faith did not allow such a level of emotional rationalization.

From the moment we left the baby in mama's care at the airport it was as if Shireen had never given birth to Shameer. She was completely committed to the journey. It was very obvious that this was to be between her and her God. As her husband I almost felt betrayed. I was jealous of Allah's place, ahead of me, in Shireen's world. But I could not, dared not, utter such heretical thoughts. I remained silent, carrying the jealousy in my heart and hoping for a return from Allah for my acceptance. My acceptance bordered on being compared to being a second husband in this existential love triangle. Maybe Allah would give me a special present as his humble servant, I thought. Although even this was not enough compensation for the jealousy I felt. It was however the only way forward for me if Shireen was to be happy and remain my wife.

The plane landed at Jeddah airport around midnight on the 20th of January 2000. The airport officials were all male. I noticed many with beards. All dressed in long thaubs and turban-clad. Yes, I thought, this is Saudi Arabia. We had arrived in the land of the wealthy oil Sheikhs, the owners of the keys to the fifth pillar of Islam, the owners of the Arabic language, the womanizers, and the land of the Muslim- American political stronghold. These were the images and thoughts that I arrived with.

Outside the airport the air was cold, the journey forward expectant. Boeta Mustapha and his wife Mariam, a couple in their sixties, travelled with us from Port Elizabeth. I knew immediately that this was to be my added burden. It started with the loading of our heavy luggage onto the roof of the bus that was to transport us to our hotel. Being the youngest and possibly strongest, I was left to load the bags on top of the roof of this old coach. With just enough strength left after the long air journey, I managed to complete the task with a false smile on my face. Shukran shukran shukran was all that I heard as I climbed up and down the ladder of the old rust bucket of a bus. Little did the shukran help my aching limbs. Why did I not pay the extra few thousand rands to travel with an organised group was one of the thoughts that kept on haunting me up and down the rungs of the ladder barely fastened on the side of what was once a bus. I was curious as to what Allah had in store for me next. It had to be worse than this with my run of luck, I thought.

We entered the city of Medina around two in the morning. It was in complete darkness. There was something mystical in the air that I could not put my finger on. My first thoughts however were about the quality of the accommodation and the possibility of a night's rest. The hotel was equivalent to a two star from where we come. Some attention to the entrance was evident. Maybe to attract would- be clientele. Only to be disappointed by the lack in further interest once you stepped out of the elevator.

Two single beds awaited our arrival. No problem I thought. This could be remedied by pushing the two metal boxes together if and when needs be. The possibility of a night's rest took priority in my thought processes at this point. The idea of rest was soon dispelled when Shireen reminded me that we should rise at four, some one and a half hours later, to perform the Tahajut prayer before the obligatory prayer at the ungodly hour of five in the morning. The thought of this insanity left me numb. I could not respond and decided to let my physical ability take over from my depleted mental state.

Two hours later we made our way along the narrow streets of Medina. The predominantly two to four storey buildings hid any sign of light that the famous Mosque of the Prophet promised. Then suddenly we heard the call of the Mu'athin. His beautiful voice pierced the quiet cold dark air as if he had practiced this for centuries. I must admit, it sent shivers down my spine. The second line of his calling had just commenced when we turned the corner and witnessed the majesty of what was to me the most mystical architectural vision that lay before. The white marble of the building and the white marble of the floor tiles lit by thousands of powerful lights must have some synergy when the two come together in an oasis of darkness. It was beautiful whilst at the same time inspired a magic that I had not witnessed anywhere before. Not even the Vatican paralleled this site, and by God did they spend money there.

Chapter 2: Memoirs of the Sacred

*„Ya ayyuha allatheena amanoola tadkhuloo buyootan ghayra
buyootikum hattatasta/nisoo watusallimoo
AAala ahliha thalikumkhayrun lakum
laAAallakum tathakkaroon"
[O you who have believed,
do not enter houses other than your own houses
until you ascertain welcome and greet their inhabitants.
That is best for you; perhaps you will be reminded.]*

I needed to enter this building for the promise of more beauty but more for the much needed warmth to ease the cold that was beginning to creep into my bones. There were so many doors to this building. I counted at least fifteen by the time I reached the closest one. Upon entering this majestic castle of Allah, the thoughts of coldness, darkness, Arab arrogance or even Shireen who had entered the lady's section through an adjacent door left my mind instantly. It was as if I was standing alone in awe of what seemed like a million pillars evenly spaced ahead of me. This religious space was filled with what seemed like a single lush Persian carpet about the size of fifty soccer fields. Only this carpet was punctuated with a million pillars equidistant apart. Serenity, equanimity and peace best describes what lay before my eyes. The miracle of architecture and interior design in pursuit of religious ambiance had found its perfection in this space.

Suddenly I remembered that the greeting of the mosque had to be performed. I had to do it right. This was my first and only opportunity. Besides, this is the mosque of the holy prophet. This is where it all began, politically at least. I faced the direction of the kiblah and very nervously raised my hands so that both thumbs touched my ears before folding my arms across my chest as we Muslims do. I had never concentrated as much in prayer as I did that day. The voice of my childhood Madrasah teacher kept echoing in my head,"Pray as if you can see Allah, but remember you cannot see Him, yet He sees you." I felt good, it felt good. I had arrived. I was going to live through history. Maybe this place too will fall as Baghdad did. I was denied then, I cannot be denied now.

I spent the next hour in this peaceful space. Not a concern in the world. At that moment I judged no one, not even myself. It felt as if the entire world was sinless. I felt compassion. For the first time in my life I felt as if my neighbour and I were one. Maybe this is what Islam was meant to bring, peace. Maybe this was salaam or nirvana or maybe even Bodhisattva status. It is hard to think of a more peaceful state. Besides, I had nothing else to do than just be. If only I could share this moment with the entire world, I thought. How selfish of Allah to give me this bliss and then deny all those I loved. Allah is all-knowing, Allah is most-merciful, Allah knows best…

The hour past too soon. When I stepped outside thousands of would be Hajjies were moving around aimlessly. The sun began to force its light through the darkness. The cold air had been replaced by comfortable warmth and the smell of tea was evident. I had to have some. But first I had to find Shireen. How was I to do this when every second woman was dressed in the same black cloak that Shireen wore? In South Africa Shireen convinced me that her black cloak was the most fashionable. It cost the family the equivalent of a month's school fees to purchase. My saving moment came when I realized that Shireen had not covered her face. She was not in purdah.

Shireen was waiting at a tea-vendor's stall not far from where I entered the mosque. Her expectant eyes met mine. She did not have to say anything. I could tell that her experiences inside was more than she had expected. I knew that she wanted a similar confirmation. My facial expressions were less obvious. I thought I had to verbalize my feelings rather than carry it around on my face. We were always fighting about this. Shireen always complained that I kept my feelings to myself. She needed more connection. I quickly whispered that I would let her know once we arrived at the hotel room.

For the next hour or so we wondered around the many small shops that were opening for business around the periphery of the grand mosque. Most of the items were made in China. These small merchants were obviously catering for the millions of pilgrims from Africa, South and East Asia where the Chinese wares had not made their way en masse. The clothes, including burkas and other Islamic garments, were also mostly imported from China, India and other manufacturing hubs such as Malaysia, the Philippines and Indonesia. How many sweat shops supplied these goods that now hold the sacred aura of Medina was my first thought. The longer I stood thinking of the irony of the meeting between global capitalism and sacrality the more the pilgrims poured into the shopping areas in search of the perfect gift to return home with.

In Cape Town, where I was raised as a child, it was customary to slip a few rands into the hands of the Gujaj when greeting and wishing them well on their nascent journey to Mecca. The reciprocal gifts that the Gujaj brings home to their loved ones are normally acquired from these small merchants in Mecca, Medina or sometimes even Jeddah. However, I have heard of merchants in Johannesburg who sell similar gifts to those returning Gujaj who had forgotten to buy enough gifts in reciprocity. At least here is a case where globalized commodities can be appreciated, albeit by unsuspecting well-wishers.

Shireen had her eyes on a number of gifts at this early stage. She was obviously attracted by the myriads of long caftans and scarves on display in the many small shops that we passed. It was hard to get her to focus on anything else. Even the tiredness of the long journey did not seem to have an effect. I, on the other hand, urgently wanted something to eat and sleep. In fact, the order did not matter as long as it was as soon as possible.

The room seemed more comfortable. Maybe the warmth of the sun eliminated the drab that welcomed us a few hours earlier. The two beds apart seemed equally comfortable as I covered myself under the two thin blankets and a sheet. I had not slept as well as this in a long while. I did not dream or did not remember if I did. The sleep was peaceful. It was a different peace. It was a peace that I had no control over. It was like nothingness. It was like a candle whose flame had been snuffed. It was like being disconnected from life itself. It was nothing like the peace I felt in the mosque a few hours earlier. That was a peace of connectedness. That was a peace of control. This was lifelessness. I relished that. I wanted more…

It was twelve thirty in the afternoon when Shireen woke me. It was time for the midday prayer. I had hardly slept for five hours. The quality must have been good as I felt restored. There were only a few minutes left before the journey back to the majestic mosque. I had still to perform the washing ritual before I could leave for the prayer. Hastily I washed my fingers, hands, arms, mouth, nostrils, ears, forehead, feet and toes. I could not help but think of the origins of this ritual. Maybe desert people had to do this as the winds blew sand constantly into their orifices. Why I had to do this I never really understood. And that at such inopportune moments like fifty seconds before the prayers. Well, I had to do it, Shireen was watching. Sometimes she can be more judgmental than Allah. I am willing to bear His wrath, hers I am careful of.

By the time we made it to the grand mosque we were welcomed by billions of sandals. It was obvious that we were late or, as Shireen would say, just in time. The Imam was about to start the prayer. This prayer is led with only the salutation "God is great" recited aloud. The rest of the prayer is read in silence by both Imam and follower. There are many more moments for contemplation during this prayer. Or as the little tradionalists would have us believe, time for Satan to play with our minds. I have always been good in this regard. My demons were silent, mostly. Soon enough the prayer ended.

On returning to the courtyard of the mosque this time, the merchants had left, their stores were closed and no tea-vendors were evident. People were making their way back to their hotels and hostels. It was siesta time. I had heard of this. We could sleep some more. I had heard once that the human propensity for sleep was second highest around midday. It made sense since what was a few hours ago the beautiful warmth of the sun was beginning to feel like the potential of a mine furnace. Besides, I thought, my brain could do with some more of that good quality sleep of a few hours before. This time, the time-god could owe me some sleep rather than the debt I felt the night before.

We made our own tea at the hotel. Rooibos tea that our well-wishers back home had placed inside Shireen's suitcase. In Cape Town the ritual is to have your family and well-wishers pack your last suitcase with small necessities as a going away gift. These would be as trivial as toilet paper, soap and often small soft bags of tea and sugar. Maybe this ritual started during the days when Gujaj travelled by sea on the long and treacherous journey to Mecca. Why in heaven's name would such a case load of inexpensive gifts be dragged twelve thousand miles when it could be purchased in Mecca for fifty dollars in total I thought? The little guy inside my head quickly answered: what was once rational is now emotional. Put differently, our forefathers are often more responsible for our actions than we are, with the caveat, that they cannot be questioned for they are long dead. This must be one of those. How powerful the dead.

This afternoon sleep lasted about an hour and a half. My neurons were satiated. I felt I could now continue the Hajj. This Hajj ritual could be likened to prayer in constant motion. Every step you take, every thought is directed by the next religious ritual to follow. It is not for the faint hearted. Sometimes I wonder why people leave it for the aged. Maybe when you are old you are less afraid. Maybe then you have wisdom on your side. Maybe then there is no choice. Maybe then God comes first. There are many old people here.

That afternoon Shireen forced me to accompany her to the market place: the clothing market place. If there was a kink in her commitment to Allah it was her strong attraction for clothing. Here Allah may have to take second place. For others, I have noticed it is cars, money, gambling or even women. For Shireen it was fashionable garments. Or more precisely garments that she deemed fashionable. I have learnt to agree with all she likes. This was the easy way out. I had less education when it came to the world of fashion. I cared less. I wondered along as if in a state of sleep walking. This was better than the covert conflict games she would play in response to any resistance I might offer to the ritual of window shopping.

Her favourite game is "yes but". She would ask me what I thought of her choice of a dress. If I answered that it was great, she would respond with yes but the colour is not right. If I disagreed with her choice she would immediately respond with "yes but" you really don't know fashion. I was always faced with a lose-lose scenario.

Shireen also displayed a frugality that suited the family budget. But when you combine frugality with the need to own a variety of clothes, a special type of behaviour comes to the front. She would move from one store to the next for hours before returning to some of the earlier ones in order to compare prices and quality. Most times she returns with her purchases for refunds as she would find a similar garment at a lower price a few hundred stores later. This behaviour upset me most. At times I end up facing the wrath of Shireen's covert conflict games for this embarrassing repetitive behaviour.

There were thousands of gift hunters. I can understand the need to find the most expensive -ooking gifts for the well-wishers back home. The more expensive the gift brought home, the greater the sincerity in the prayer by the well-wishers for the Gujaj. I have experienced the beautiful comments and remarks made by well-wishers when receiving seemingly expensive gifts from returning Gujaj. There is a distinct kindness in the voice and a humble demeanor of deference in the recipient of the gift. This peculiar behavior becomes more pronounced the more expensive the gift is.

The Gujaj are also keenly aware of the amount of money that was given them by the well-wishers back home. The stipend that is placed into the hand of the Gujaj on that last formal greeting is folded into as small a note as possible then placed with great care into the hand of the Gujaj. The Gujaj thanks the giver then quickly places it into his pocket as if it will have anonymity amongst the hundreds of other small notes already lying in wait in the pocket. As soon as the opportunity arises to assess the gifts, the Gujaj quickly makes a mental note of who gave the most and who only partook in the ritual of gift giving by using money as mere tokenism. These misers run the risk of receiving one of those gifts bought in packs ten. I have been that unlucky.

The rest of the week was spent in this routine: prayer and shopping. How pleased Shireen was. The peace and contentment on her face was one I had not seen for such a sustained period in our relatively short marriage of four years. I was amazed at the bliss religion and material brought when combined. It was all the will of Allah. Allah knows best…Allah is most gracious … Allah is most merciful.

Chapter 3: The Sufi

"Allahu nooru assamawatiwal-ardi mathalu noorihi kamishkatin feehamisbahun almisbahu fee zujajatinazzujajatu kaannaha kawkabun durriyyunyooqadu min shajaratin mubarakatin zaytoonatin lasharqiyyatin wala gharbiyyatin yakadu zaytuhayudee-o walaw lam tamsas-hu narun noorun AAalanoorin yahdee Allahu linoorihi man yashao wayadribuAllahu al-amthala linnasi wallahubikulli shay-in AAaleem"
[Allah is the Light of the heavens and the earth. The example of His light is like a niche within which is a lamp, the lamp is within glass, the glass as if it were a pearly [white] star lit from [the oil of] a blessed olive tree, neither of the east nor of the west, whose oil would almost glow even if untouched by fire. Light upon light. Allah guides to His light whom He wills. And Allah presents examples for the people, and Allah is Knowing of all things.]

We never missed a prayer in Jama'a in eight consecutive days. Shireen and I were covertly competing against each other spiritually. Or rather, I was trying to keep up to her commitment to salat five times per day in communal prayer inside the mosque of the holy prophet. I was getting into the routine surprisingly easier than I had at first thought. Back home people assumed, because I wore a long thaub and sported an unkempt beard, that I followed the five daily prayers religiously. For me it was more about the collective social environment. In other words, I was accepted and judged by my friends and family by the unkemptness of my facial hair and by my outward display of humility. For me religion was equal to society. I was worshipping society.

The idea of a monotheistic deity was what my society insisted on. However, there was no iconography of Allah. In fact, I am told, that any physical depiction of Allah or even his prophet Muhammad was an act of heresy. More precisely, the name Allah is an amalgam of the two Arabic words Ilah (God) and the definite article al (the)."The God" (Allah) is said to be omnipotent and omniscient. Allah is known by his ninety-nine attributes or titles which include amongst others, the greatest, the most-merciful and the most-forgiving. Allah is known through language only. It was easy for me to accept this language; I was socialized with this language. I am a product of my forefathers' constructed realities. I suspended any judgments on these existential questions. It seemed safer. I continued to worship society.

It was four twenty in the afternoon that I entered through one of the majestic doors of the mosque for the late-afternoon prayer. Carefully I removed my sandals making sure to place them in the furthest corner of the thousand rows of racks. I could not afford to lose this pair. Even though they were inexpensive, they were comfortable. I was warned in advance of the sandal thieves. I opted for caution.

As I turned to look outside into the courtyard one last time to see if I could catch a glimpse of Shireen, her eyes met mine. Not Shireen's eyes, the eyes of a stranger. She was approaching the entrance from a distance holding onto the arm of a blind old man. He was feeling his way forward with a white cane in his right hand and the woman holding on to his left arm. Her eyes communicated with mine. Help my father into the mosque was her request. I waited for them to reach the entrance. I placed my hand in the same place where she had held onto him. I could still feel the warmth of her hand as if she had not let go. We said nothing to each other. Her gaze was lowered, my mind restricted, his mind with Allah.

This was a holy man. Maybe a saint, maybe he was a Sufi. Ordinary he was not. He wore a long off-white coat that almost touched the ground. The hood of his coat was hanging neatly at the nape of his neck. There was a rope tied around his waist. His shoes were rather exotic. They were yellow with the front tips upwardly pointing as if reaching for the heavens. My eyes were fixed on these shoes as he removed them. He placed them on the shoe rack in front of us. He placed them on the middle shelf without a care for the sandal thieves. Who would have the courage to wear these I thought. Maybe only a blind person would have that courage. Maybe only a Sufi would have that confidence. No not I.

He folded his white stick and depended increasingly on me to guide him to the front rows of the mosque. It was relatively empty still. As we moved forward I could hear him repeating the phrase, "Allah hu Akbar, Allah hu Akbar" with every step he took. I found a place for us some twenty meters away from the mimba. As we sat in waiting I touched his hand to reassure him I would stay with him until the end of the prayer. I had to. How was he to find his way back to those exotic shoes, I thought. For a while the thought of him being an unknowing shoe thief crossed my mind. Maybe to him all sandals and shoes belonged to Allah. Maybe I was too occupied with material. Maybe he saw the world differently. Maybe the blind serve Allah differently. Maybe they also serve who mainly serve through patience.

During the prayer he did something that I had never witnessed in salat before. He wrote the name of Allah in the air as we sat awaiting the Imam to conclude with the salutations. He did it a number of times. I then remembered that this was the closest we can get to an iconic depiction of Allah: The name Allah itself in written form. How could I deny him his God? What else does he have but this icon? We humans need symbols, we cannot live without symbols. Could there be an Allah without our symbols? I suspend my judgment. Allah knows best…

Immediately after the completion of the prayers I took the role of the guide. Allah hu Akbar was all I could faintly hear every step of the way. He was special; he did not need me or Allah's servants. He was leading me. How blind I was. He knew exactly where to find his fashion sneakers. I searched for mine. We left the building. There she was, the lady with the talking eyes. She said shukran yet uttered not a word. He pulled me back and made a prayer. I knew immediately that the prayer was a gift. Not a gift that needed reciprocity. He wanted nothing. He had his words. He had his icons.

His prayer remained in my mind as if etched in diamonds. I understood what he had said. He spewed out a sentence that had a million meanings for me. I smiled as I stood in the courtyard thinking about what had just transpired. I was rewarded for my gift to this blind man. I was rewarded for being the guide. I wanted reward. I would never have admitted it. Then the blind man's message echoed again. Only this time the message was unexpected. It echoed vividly in my mind,"You are a nothing, don't think you are special, you are only the instrument of Allah". I was used. I was used by the grand metaphysic. I did not mind. I liked it.

Shireen will hear of this.

I wandered down the street on my way to the hotel. I smiled. I was happy. Sitting down on my bed I decided to search for the blind man's Arabic verse in our small Islamic encyclopedia that Shireen insisted on bringing along. I had to carry it. The burden of carriage and interpretation were both mine. The final validation of the interpretation belonged to her. Be that as it may, I opened the single volume tome in search of the sacred verse. I could hardly believe what had just happened. I opened the book on a page that contained that very verse. What were my chances of finding the verse on the first opening of the text? This was magic. I was scared yet hungry in anticipation for more signs. This time the message was different. It read,"Pray in front of Allah as if you can see Allah, but remember you cannot, yet He sees you". I knew this. I needed to put it into practice.

An hour and a half later I was back at the sacred house of Allah standing shoulder to shoulder with my brothers from Afghanistan and Timbuktu. Yes we were brothers in Islam. I would do things for these strangers that I would deny my biological siblings. Ideas are often stronger than blood. Patiently we waited for the Imam to start the salat ritual. I focused on Allah ahead of me as if I could see her. I accepted that she could see me. I raised my hands after the Imam gave his signal. I folded my arms across my chest as we Muslims do. Instantly my spirit left my body. I found myself flying over Yemen like a superman character. The Yemenites were in the same prayer as our Jama'a in Medina, only further advanced. Within a second I hovered over Egypt and witnessed a similar group of people in salat. A second later I was flying over the holy city of Makkah. This time the people had completed their salat. Not even a second later I travelled along an imaginary line that stretched from the Kabah to the highest heavens. Here I witnessed men and women dressed in white walking around an extension of the Kabah. It was as if the Kabah found its foundations on earth with the roof of this tall building now evident to me in the highest heavens. As on earth, these pilgrims dressed in white moved in unison around the highest part of the extended Kabah. All the while I was hovering in the air watching humans circumambulate the Kabah.

All of a sudden a black wind blew past at supersonic speed. I was touched by this wind. I had never felt such calm. When I opened my eyes I was back in Medina standing in line with the rest of my brothers listening to the beautiful voice of Sheikh Sudais. It was as if I had left for no more than a second. My experience was real. I believed it. I closed my eyes and tried it again. Off I went along the same journey experiencing the magic for a second time. Only this time it seemed twice as fast. When I opened my eyes I was back in Medina next to my Afghanistani brother. He had to be Afghan. His left foot kicked against mine on two occasions. It was hard as rocks. This was the foot of a Mujahedeen. This was the foot of a Bedouin fighter. Is this what the American soldiers have to contend with? Is this what the metro sexual male has to contend with? I felt empathy for those with pedicure wants. I felt sorry for the American soldiers.

I was back on ground zero. I was back in the majestic mosque. I could not repeat the magic no matter how hard I tried. There was something special that happened to me. I was convinced. I did not have to convince anyone. The evidence was in my body. I felt ten times stronger than I did before this special journey through the air. I felt I could physically fight ten men at the same time. My mind was stronger.

I left the mosque in a state of ecstasy. I was drunk with magic. Allah had given me Hull. I did not ask for it. It was His gift. I was convinced He expected no return. I had to tell Shireen. I was afraid she might be jealous. Why me, Kimal Baig, hypocrite, apostate, charlatan, munafiq…I judged myself. I questioned Allah's choice. The evidence was with me. The strength was undeniable. The intellect matched the ten-fold increase in physical strength. I had a conversation with myself about all of this. I was definitely not deluded. The test came almost immediately.

While waiting for Shireen outside the mosque to share the holy news with her, I saw a woman who looked like my mother standing a few meters from me. The woman was in tears. The resemblance was strong. It was my mother's older sister Hanim. She was very happy to see me. On enquiring why she was weeping I learnt that the Hajj agent that had brought her and her young daughter, Nuraan, on pilgrimage had made off with their life savings. He had taken their accommodation money for the pilgrimage and had disappeared. Aunty Hanim pointed out that she had seen him enter a building some fifty meters from where we were standing. Hurriedly I made my way to the four storey dive. He was with a friend on the third floor. I knocked on his door like the riot police used to do in South Africa during the '76 uprisings. His friend opened the door shivering at the sight of me standing there with not one hair of fear on my head. I was more than ready to take him, his friend and all their sisters' husbands. I had never felt this confident before. I could tell they were not going to even attempt to argue with me. He handed me my aunt's money with the promise that he would never do this to anyone again. I said nothing. My aunt was happy; she could continue her journey with dignity. She could continue her journey with me.

We were six in our party now, Shireen and I, Boeta Mustapha and his wife aunty Mariam, aunty Hanim and her daughter Nuraan. What did I do to deserve this extra burden? Why did I not pay the extra few thousand rands to go with an organised tour group? What else did Allah have in store for me? I remembered the prayer of the blind man, "You are a nothing, don't think you are special, you are only the instrument of Allah". Maybe I was being used by Allah to help these slaves of His. Allah is most gracious…Allah is most merciful…Allah knows best.

Chapter 4: The Hijra Reversed

> *"Labbaik Allahumma Labbaik. Labbaik,*
> *La Shareek Laka, Labbaik Innal Hamdah,*
> *Wan Nematah, Laka wal Mulk,*
> *La Shareek Laka Labbaik"*
> [Here I am at Thy service O Lord, here I am.
> Here I am at Thy service and Thou hast no partners.
> Thine alone is All Praise and All Bounty,
> and Thine alone is The Sovereignty. Thou hast no partners.]

Leaving the city of Medina left me with a feeling of sadness. I said goodbye to the graves of the Ansar and the Muhajirun. I witnessed many crying at these veneration sites. I witnessed the Shi'i followers display sadness at these holy graves of their Imams. The sadness that could fuel a revolution, and tears that could fill the tributaries of the Tigress and Euphrates. I witnessed emotions that Sunni followers would never be able to match. They [The Shi'i] mourn their dead. They worship their dead. The Saudi asgaries whip them in jealousy. The Sunnis bemoan their passion. The Shi'I's ancestors are more important to them than mine are to me. How powerful their dead.

I said goodbye to the battlefields of old. The prophet had fought there. We venerated these shrines. I relived the battles. I said goodbye to Uhud and Khandag. I internalized the events. I hated the tribes, even the Banu-Nadir, the Banu-Qainuka and the Banu Quraiza. I had to. I learnt to love Salman Farsi. I learnt to hate Abu Sufyan. I learnt the art of trench warfare. I learnt to appreciate the value of wits.

I experienced history and historical engineering. I witnessed the demolition of the mosque of Abu Bakr. I witnessed the demolition of the mosque of Umar. I witnessed the demolition of the mosque of Ali. I witnessed the demolition of shirk. I witnessed Wahabi ideological engineering. I witnessed the union of political and religious ideals. You cannot revere stone. You cannot revere history. You cannot revere the dead. You cannot have your own ideas. These mosques had to be destroyed by the Wahabis. They were to build new mosques on these sites. Maybe then the Shi'i will stop. There were just too many who believed in venerating stone. I said goodbye with sadness. I said goodbye to magic.

Both Shireen and I had our special long towels that would be our pilgrim's dress in place as we boarded the diesel bus en route to Makkah. The ritual is to be dressed in these special cloths, Ighraam, when entering the holy city of Makkah. The holy city has a few gates of entry many kilometers from its centre. Between these gates and the Makkan centre, the Kabah, lie millions of square meters of desert sand. Nothing but sand and heat separates the visitor from the house of Abraham.

We entered the gate through Bir Ali. The bus stopped here in order for us to don the long towels. The men's change rooms were closest to the bus stop. We were all equal with these uniforms. Not even my long Thaub could buy me the extra sacredness that my friends bestowed on it. Shireen's expensive black cloak lost its sacred value. There was a leveling of the sacred playing field. The towel cloths were kept in place by a single safety pin. We were allowed nothing more. How funny Boeta Mustapha looked. His left boob was clearly showing. We were all dressed alike. All we had were our towels and our demeanor. The towels were all the same. We could only be distinguished by our demeanor. What games were to be played from here? Some of us need material. Some of us are lost without it. The God must be smiling. The challenge lay ahead. Labbaik Allahumma Labbaik…

The journey took a few hours from Bir Ali to Makkah. Some of the travelers were showing their frustrations. The vinyl seats became increasing uncomfortable as the journey progressed. People were anxious. People were nervous. They were about to enter the city of Makkah. They had to know their rituals. They had to know their prayers. For most of us Allah only understood Arabic. For most of us Allah only allowed one way. For most it cost a life's savings. For most it was the only opportunity. We had to do it right, our friends were watching. Only Allah knows our intentions, our friends were judging our actions. Only Allah can judge. Our friends are watching for Him. I was afraid of my friends.

We entered the city of Makkah. It was different from Medina. It was alive. It was busy. We needed to greet the Kabah. We needed to see the Kabah. We needed ritual before sleep. Shireen and I separated from the group in order to do it right. We entered through the gate that was said to be the same gate that the prophet used on his triumphant return from Medina only fourteen hundred years earlier. We wanted to follow his example. We wanted to follow the dead.

There it was, the Kabah, only many times bigger than we had imagined. It was positioned in the centre of a huge coliseum. This mosque was bigger than that of Medina. It was busier. More money had been spent here. It was awe-inspiring. It lacked the calm of Medina. It belonged to the pagans of past. It belonged to the Sabbeans. In the past people had moved around this sacred building clothed only with a smile. Abraham and his son Ishmael had built it. They sowed their seed.

Their offspring were present. We were present. Our family was present. Shireen did not need Shameer. I did not need her. She did not need me. We were here, each person accountable for their own salvation. We had arrived.

The ritual of circumambulation had to be performed. I decided to speak to Allah in Afrikaans. I was certain the God would understand. My God is all-knowing. Carefully and slowly Shireen and I walked around the Kabah, side by side. She armed with her Arabic, me with my Afrikaans. I could see the commitment in her eyes. I could see the struggle on her face. Her Arabic was poor, my Afrikaans was good. I asked Allah for forgiveness for my wife's inability to understand the Arabic rhymes. I was certain He understood me. I only had my demeanor. I could use nothing else.

When we arrived at the last corner of this cubic structure we were welcomed by the black stone. I needed to rub my hands on it. The masses of pilgrims had equal wants. It was too difficult this time, maybe next time I thought. We made our prayers facing the door of the Kabah. No little demons tried to distract me this time. Immediately thereafter we made our way to the final ritual before we could find a hotel, hopefully for the rest of our stay in Makkah. This ritual is known as the Sai. The ritual involves the to-and-fro walking between mount Safa and mount Marwa. We are told this is where Abraham's second wife Hajar ran to-and-fro in search of water to quest the thirst of her infant son Ishmael. I could never understand why Abraham would leave his young son and wife to fend for themselves without water in the desert. Allah knows best...

To-and-fro Shireen and I walked, seven times, to fulfill the Sai. Again I did not remember the Arabic. I stuck with Afrikaans. Shireen remained with her Arabic. She did not waiver. Her faith was stronger than mine. After the Sai we made our way to the rest of the group as agreed. The greeting of the Kabah was over. We could now search for a reasonably priced hotel; two stars would be great I thought. Maybe this time we might even be blessed with a double bed. It did not matter to me. I was content. I carried the experience of the special journey with me. I was strong. I would be called upon to be used at any moment. I was ready. Allah understood my Afrikaans. I was convinced.

Boeta Mustapha and I were left to negotiate with the hotel manager. It was obvious that money was all important. Our brothers and sisters in the group were concerned that Boeta Mustapha or I would negotiate a special deal for ourselves. They did not trust us even though they did not say so. They did not have to. I can understand. This was the life's savings of some. This was the jealousy of others. We negotiated a price for the duration of our stay up to the last week of the Hajj. We would have to move out for that week as the price of a bed quadrupled in that week. I now understood why they only had single beds. It had an economic function. Other human concerns could not compete against the greed for money. The hotel manager quickly pointed out that there were other hotels not far from this well-positioned one star abode. He would gladly accommodate us in these hotels on the slopes of Makkah. The price seemed right. We had to confer with our friends. We could not make a decision. It had to be transparent. Allah would not judge us, our friends would. This time we opted to worship our friends.

By this time our party had increased by four. Two more couples from South Africa had joined us immediately after the Sai ritual. They were friends of Boeta Mustapha from Port Elizabeth. The men were more willing than their women to voice their distrust. We had to find accommodation; the light of day was but a couple of hours away. We were tired. We were desperate to sleep and settle. Our friends decided that we were to take this accommodation for a day and decide thereafter. I was not sure whether the hotel manager would give us the same rate for a day-to-day transaction. We had to negotiate again; our friends did not trust us.

The jovial hotel manager was quite willing to accept the new terms. How else, there were only a few hours before daylight. Money found its rightful place in the rationalization process. Money could buy much here. Where we lived would determine our status amongst our fellow Gujaj from South Africa. This dive that we could afford was certainly not going to raise our status amongst the holy from back home. This was the unspoken concern of the new members of the group. Aunty Hanim and cousin Nuraan were equally concerned about the status component but opted to stay with Kimal the giant killer. They did not have to say anything; the look on their faces said it all when they entered the room that mother and daughter had to share. I knew their financial status. They could barely afford anything better. I understood their plight. They would be judged by their friends. I convinced them that all would be fine. I convinced them to look at the bigger picture. They bought my rationalizations. I had learnt at an early stage of my life that all of life was about selling one's actions to oneself. I had learnt at an early age that all of life was about selling your actions to others. Allah did not matter. Your friends mattered.

Early the next morning our new-found friends departed to a better hotel a few hundred meters from our hotel. We decided to remain. We rationalized our actions. They rationalized theirs. I was told by Boeta Mustapha to visit their up- market abode to compare our dwelling with his. It was no better than our hotel. I could not see the difference. They were convinced. They rationalized their better abode. All was well. Our original group decided to remain with the initial agreement. The manager was excited. He wanted his money. We paid.

It was our first day in Makkah. We started the day with the Morning Prayer at five. There is something ripe and satisfying about rising before the sun. It feels as if you have a head start over all sentient beings. This time the Grand Mosque of Makkah seemed many times more peaceful than when we arrived less than twelve hours earlier. I suspect this to be the case as many find it difficult to rise this early. I suspect that many who stay away from this prayer live outside the eyes of their friends and neighbours. I suspect many of these pilgrims live in five star hotels where their friends and neighbours cannot watch them. We were watched. We had to be there. It was a luxury to be there. Only those with the most melodious voices are allowed to lead the prayers. And during this Morning Prayer the longest verses of the Qur'an were recited. It was enjoyable.

Immediately thereafter we left the mosque with the intention of buying breakfast on the street. The tea-vendors were out, steam rising from their trolleys. They all served the same tea. No Rooibos here. It was all yellow label tea with cream instead of milk. They had found a perfect recipe. After my first cup, I wanted no other combination. It only cost the equivalent of thirty American cents. These tea-vendors were constantly busy. I enquired from one vendor of Pakistani origin about the profitability of his venture. Without hesitation he quickly informed me that his was a partnership with a Saudi national. He was not allowed to operate independently. This said, during the week of Hajj he made enough money to spend the rest of the year serving Allah fulltime. He had been doing this for twenty years. He wanted nothing else in life. He said that his position in Makkah was due to the mercy of Allah. He rarely returns to Pakistan as the sacrality of the holy mosque and his good fortune offered him this comfortable lifestyle. The marriage of capital and religion brings contentment most times.

Shireen and I sat on the sidewalk of a street leading directly from the main entrance. We savoured our yellow label tea and soft rolls that we purchased for around the same price as the tea. We were doing as the Germans do: Leutesehen. Watching people was a favorite pastime of mine. This was especially pleasurable since many South Africans strolled by. I could tell they were from South Africa as many spoke in Afrikaans. Most of them were from the Cape. They have a distinct accent when speaking this patois Dutch. It is not beautiful. I liked it. It made me feel closer to home. I even recognized some from Cape Town. Ouw my bro, what's up, one of them remarked in recognizing me. It's all good, I replied.

We were seated for about fifteen minutes when a lady with a baby on her arms approached us for money. She must have been from North Africa, she was black. Immediately I thought of the third pillar of Islam: to give zakah. Giving the women a Saudi Riyal or two did not constitute an act of zakah, but rather an act of charity or sadaqa. Zakah is what we owed our poor. Zakah was based on one's net worth on an annual basis. Zakah belonged to the poor. This lady wanted charity. I handed her a couple of Riyals. I felt good. I felt I did something for Allah. I expected a return even though I would never say it. However, as soon as her friends saw my kindness, a second, then a third young woman were around me. I quickly handed them all I had only to be swamped by a horde of women demanding more. It was as if a million flies had discovered a dead fish. The more I tried to tell them that I had no more money with me, the less they seemed interested in my lies. It took at least ten minutes to shake them off. From that point on I decided to keep my charity private. Shireen stayed by my side throughout the ordeal. As we walked away from this tirade we passed a billboard that read, "It is not appropriate to beg in Islam". This almost sounded like "Please do not feed the birds". The Saudi authorities had invoked some hadith of Bukhari that reports that the prophet was against begging. I was not going to believe this billboard. I thought about a story that a South Asian friend had told me. He said that in Delhi he had seen a billboard that read, "If you're not trying, you're dying". I was keen to experience more of Saudi's social world. I was keen to experience Hajj.

The morning sleep was good. I could feel the warmth of the sun enter through the hotel room. I fell asleep only to be woken by what felt like jahannam. You have no idea what fifty degrees Celsius feels like until you experience the desert heat of Saudi Arabia. Our budget did not allow for air conditioning. I climbed into the shower for some reprieve. Shireen suggested we leave immediately for the grand mosque. At least there we could get some air conditioning and zamzam. I now understood why our hotel manager seemed so eager for us to commit to spend the rest of our Hajj at his old hotel. I would have paid twice the price if I had known that Allah's sun was to be so merciless. At least the Saudi tea was good.

We all rationalize. We are all human, only the God is divine, Allah knows best.

Chapter 5: The Black Stone

> *"Ina awal bayt assesa le alnas la a the be baka"*
> *[The Kabah is the first house of worship created by Allah S.W.T]*

Shireen and I made our way to the Gharam, grand mosque, in search of air conditioning, zamzam and holiness. We wanted to see the Kabah during the day. We wanted to circumambulate again. Shireen made her intensions clear from the moment we left the hotel. She wanted to walk around the Kabah as many times as humanly possible for the duration of her stay in Makkah. The Gharam was a completely different sight to behold during the day. Artificial lighting has an effect I am told. The Kabah was surrounded with thousands of square meters of marble. Yes, pure marble imported from Italy I would later learn. No expense was spared. The white marble was beautifully contrasted against the black cloth, embroidered with pure gold thread, which covered the sacred house of Abraham. The door of the Kabah was made from solid gold and was big enough for a ten foot giant to enter without having to bend his neck. A few meters from the Kabah, cast in stone, was a display unit that housed the footprint of Abraham. His shoe size must have been around a humungous 23UK in our language. I now understood why the door was so huge; Abraham must have been a giant. On the front right corner was the al-Hajar al-Aswad, famously known as the Black Stone. I could not get to touch it, even this time, the competition was too stiff. However, I was determined to do so at least once. If only I could get close enough.

We had to view the Kabah from a distance as there was a constant crowd of at least twenty thousand people moving around the Kabah in the ritual of tawwaaf (circumambulation). There is something to be said about moving in a circle and praying. The circular movement of the body while in prayer brings spiritual ecstasy for some. I have witnessed the twirling dervishes, the Hindu swamis, some Zionists African Independent Church members and Iranian Sufis moving in circles when wanting to achieve spiritual ecstasy. For a while I thought of my youth in the children's park in my neighbourhood. The swings were my sibling's favourite item in the park. I preferred the bus. It rotated on a single axis in a circular motion. We would push it as fast as possible and would end up drunk and disoriented. Maybe the circular motion of the body with rhythmic chanting could achieve a similar state, I thought. Only this time I could be drunk with love for the God or myself. I suddenly moved faster in search of this dizzy state. Shireen was caught unawares by the sudden increase in my gate. I was not alone; I saw many moving at high speeds through the masses. Maybe they were aware of this dizzy intoxication. Shireen was furious with me when she eventually caught up. I explained to her that the faster we moved the more revolutions we would be able to complete. I have heard returning pilgrims boast of the many hundreds of tawwaafs they had completed while in Makkah. The more you complete, the more the potential pilgrims back home admired them. Shireen bought this line of thinking. We humans rationalize our actions.

If I thought I was moving fast I was proven wrong almost immediately for fast passing me was a team of four strong black men, muscles bulging, carrying an older lady in a cart above their heads. This team was virtually running with the cart. I was convinced that the lady upstairs would be intoxicated after the first few revolutions. I was later told that you paid handsomely for this luxury and that the speed had more to do with getting the next pilgrim on board than with intoxication. These black rickshaw runners earned a fortune by running the frail around the Kabah. There was always a financial motivation. Money could buy almost anything here.

After many circumambulations, in sets of seven, I achieved my goal of touching the Black Stone albeit for a brief second. As we made our way along the last leg of the tawwaaf, I asked Allah to give me the strength to muscle my way through the masses. Shireen was caught unawares. I left her side without consultation and aimed my direction at the Black Stone. I was amazed at the ease with which the crowd parted in front of me. It was as if the Blind Sufi with the yellow shoes pushed them aside to pave an easy route for me to the stone. The encounter was swift. The stone had a smooth glass-like feel. I made a special prayer in Afrikaans during that second as the force of the crowd pushed me away. I didn't mind. I had done it. My status among the group would be elevated. My status would have reached even higher levels had I kissed it. Shireen was waiting only a few meters away for me. The admiration in her eyes said it all. We humans venerate stone. We humans become intoxicated with the veneration of stone.

I had touched the most important stone in the world. This stone is deemed so important that people had stolen it from the Kabah in the past. This was a special stone. It fell from the heavens. It is the connection between those up there and us down here. These stones are rare. These meteorites are rare.

Shireen and I had a paper cup of zamzam water after my holy achievement of touching the Black Stone. This was water from the well that gushed forth when Hajar ran to-and-fro between Safa and Marwa. It is holy water. It was blessed from the beginning. It needed no further blessing. There is something milky in its taste. Ishmael had drunk some of this. The prophet had drunk of this. I had to drink some of this. We worship the dead. I worshipped the dead.

We had just satisfied our thirst for both water and holiness when the call to start the afternoon prayer sounded. Suddenly I was left with a serious dilemma. Who was to lead the prayer? Was he a Sunni? Was he a Shi'ite? Was he Wahabi? Female it could not be. But more importantly, how was I to follow a leader with a different Islamic doctrine to mine? I had to make a decision quickly. He could not be a Shi'ite as the prayer leaders earlier had not prostrated on stones. These Saudi Imams could not be of the same school of thought as I was as the earlier prayers differed from how I had been taught, albeit in minor detail. They could not have been from any of the other three major schools of thought in Sunni Islam, as I knew those. He had to be Wahabi. What was I to do? Shireen had already made her way to the women's section. She was not my concern. I decided to follow the Wahabi. I saw no other protest. I followed the Wahabi. I followed the crowd. We follow society. We worship society. This society was worshipping the God. The clerics at home will hear of this.

After the Wahabi Imam completed the prayers we were told to stay for the burial service of one of the pilgrims. Here the Wahabis waste no time in burial. The dead are buried within hours of their final breath. Those who carry the dead to the graveyard do so in a canter. There are no tombstones here. The Wahabis are less inclined than the Shi'i or other Sunnis to venerate stone. The Wahabis insisted on their way. They have graveyards without headstones. You lose your identity in Wahabi culture once you die. I have noticed that those who are less concerned about their dead are many times more concerned about the material of this world. I have noticed the Protestants. I have noticed the Jews. I now noticed the Wahabis.

After the prayers for the dead – and I was certain that the dead had been interred by the time the prayer was done – Shireen and I met at the main entrance of the Gharam. I was bare foot. My cheap beach tongs had been stolen. I made my way along the main street as fast as I could to collect some cash to replace them. To my chagrin I had a blister on my right foot by the time I arrived at the one star hotel without the air conditioning. Nothing major to worry myself over was my first thought. Within half an hour I had purchased a second cheap pair of sandals. They were not as comfortable as my previous pair. They would eventually fit I told myself. They all eventually do.

By the end of the evening prayers my right foot was so infected that I could not step on it. I was furious when I realized my myopia. I looked around to confirm my suspicions. Yes, I was right. People spat all over the place. It was a cultural necessity for some to drop their phlegm including parts of their alveoli on the streets and sidewalks. I must have stepped in a few hundred different sputums in my haste to buy the new pair. In that second that the phlegm theory crossed my mind there must have been at least a dozen men and at least half a dozen women taking pride in depositing their mucous balls as they were walking past me. I have never tried this in public. For a while I was tempted to do so in retaliation. I opted for antibiotics instead.

My foot slowed me down significantly. As the days past, my disrespect for the sidewalk phlegmers increased. They were not my favourite pilgrims. I was convinced the God would not have approved. There were so many of them that I now believed that there are different levels in janah (heaven). There had to be. In all fairness the God could not place all his creations – good and semi-good - in the same place. I was aiming for a level different from these sidewalk phlegmers. It did not matter whether the level was higher or lower, as long as the phlegmers did not share sidewalks with me.

Not being very mobile, I opted to spend my free time from ritual hours doing my favourite pastime: Leutesehen (people watching). There were at least one hundred countries represented here. Only Muslims are allowed to enter Makkah. This is one place that my non-Muslim friends would have to consult me about. I was keen to pick out the Saudi national from the many Pakistanis, Bangladeshis and other South Asians. After a few inquiries I learnt that the tell-tale sign of the Saudi national was the red checkered scarf that they sport. They are certain to iron the front tip of the scarf into a sharp edge. Without intimate discussion, in Arabic, I would have no way of distinguishing between the South Asians and the Arabs. The colour of their skin wouldn't help as many Saudis were Negroid and for most it would be almost impossible for the untrained eye as mine to distinguish them as many looked South Asian. I had to find other markers of identity. I had not been here long enough to make educated observations. Leutesehen, because of my infected foot, had a purpose after all. Immediately I searched for the red checkered scarves that were perfectly ironed.

There were many, but not so ubiquitous that I could find them that easily. I thought I would spot them at first, and then ask a second and third opinion to check if my observations were correct. After a few spots and observations I became good at it. There was almost an obsession with the Arab national to secure the checkered scarf over their heads. The pointed front was always present. The individuals that I watched were even fidgeting with their scarves during prayer. I was under the impression that they were to focus their minds on Allah during prayer. It seemed that the pre-occupation with the sharp edge had priority over the prayer. I was not going to mention my observations to my friends as I was supposed to be in equal concentration at the time. As an ideal type, these Arab Saudis were very neat and seemed concerned about their appearances. They did not stay long after the prayers and always seemed hurried as if they had to return to their places of work or homes. I never witnessed the Saudi male escort his wife to or from the Gharam. He was always alone or in the company of a friend. And in all cases that I witnessed, based on my criteria above, a friend of Saudi origin.

The most populace nation here was Indonesia. Indonesians were easy to spot and observe as they often sported the name of their country and travel agents on their shirts. The Tabang Hajjies were the most prevalent. It was not uncommon to see couples walking hand-in-hand toward the Gharam and in some cases the husband would pray next to his wife. This observation was not mine alone. Shireen had mentioned on a couple of times how cute this was. Boeta Mustapha was appalled at this irreligiosity. The Indonesians did not seem to mind. They seemed quite accustomed to praying with their women. I wondered if their women led them in prayer. I wondered what Boeta Mustapha would have to say about that possibility. I had never been led in prayer by a woman. I wondered if the God would accept such a prayer. I wondered if the God would accept my prayer if I was to be led by a woman. I cannot answer…only the God can.

Then there were the Pakistanis, the Indians and the Bangladeshis. I had to group them together as I could not distinguish between them. They seemed to be more at home here in the great city of Makkah. They seemed even more numerous than the Indonesians. They are the cleaners, the hotel staff, the road sweepers and the cooks. I was convinced every Saudi owned a South Asian. They were here as workers for the Saudis. My first thought was about the ratio of worker male to worker female as I saw very few women working in public. Were these migrant workers divorced from their women for extended periods? What were the consequences of such an abnormal lifestyle or abnormal as I viewed it? As the days progressed I was inclined to believe that their social relationships in the overtly male-centered Makkah to be causing them some inconvenience. They were constantly staring at Shireen. It became so bad that Shireen decided, by herself and a little by my persuasion, to cover her face in purdah. My friends remarked that Shireen had attained a higher level of spirituality and hence decided on purdah. Little did they know that Shireen could no longer endure the lusty eyes of the thousands of workers who opted for money and celibacy instead of family life. Money trumps emotions most times. It is especially beautiful when money and sacrality meet. If you think I am telling half-truths, ask a South Asian migrant worker in Saudi Arabia. I have met many who only visit their wives every fifth year. It is all the will of Allah…Allah is most merciful…Allah knows best.

Chapter 6: The Cave

> *"Iqra' bismi rabbikal lazii khalaq khalaqal*
> *insaana min 'alaq iqra' wa Rabbukal akram*
> *Allazii 'allama bil –qalam"*
> *[Recite with the name of your Lord Who created.*
> *He made man from the clot of blood. Recite, for your Lord*
> *is the Most Generous. Who taught writing by the pen.]*

On the sixth day of our stay in Makkah our group decided to visit the cave of Hira on Jabal (Mount) Nur. This was where the first verses of the Qur'an were revealed to the prophet Mohammad. The infection in my foot had subsided and I was excited to visit this historic venue. Around ten in the morning our bus set out to the holy site. There are thousands of buses here, all fueled by diesel. These Saudis obviously have no concern about fuel as there were only six of us in a bus that could easily seat sixty people. For a while I was concerned about Allah's environment and the effects of the toxic gases that diesel combustion produces. No wonder I thought, every second pilgrim becomes a phlegmer here. With all the money that is generated by the Hajj could these tourist moguls not spend a few riyals to improve the transportation system? This year there were reported to be in excess of four million pilgrims. All had to travel by bus. And during the week of the Hajj rituals almost all of the four million pilgrims had to be accommodated on a toxic diesel polluter. Simple arithmetic tells me that I would not be far off if I said there would be around sixty six thousand buses to pull off that feat. Now imagine sixty six thousand toxic spewing buses all revved up in a fifteen kilometer radius. The holy city becomes the most profane carbon jungle anywhere on earth.

I was convinced the God would not be happy with this destructive technology. Yes my friends, money is all important here.

I quickly focused my mind on the journey ahead and the sacrality it would offer. Shireen was rather quiet. She had youth and physical strength on her side. I had the strength of the mystic on my side. The rest of our group, except for cousin Nuraan, had wisdom and old age on theirs. I had not seen the size of Mount Hira yet and was wondering about the physical task ahead. Boeta Mustapha had trouble overcoming the two flights of stairs at our hotel. I was concerned for him. I was concerned for those who leave Hajj until old age. I was concerned for those who hedge their eschaton against age. There are many old people here.

We arrived at the famous Mount Hira. It was about half the size of Table Mountain. There was no way any of my friends, besides Nuraan, would be able to reach the top. The famous cave was located about twenty metres on the other side of the mountain. We had to walk to the top and then climb another twenty meters down on the other side in order to visit the cave. Boeta Mustapha and his wife didn't even give it a second thought. They were not going to even attempt the impossible. Nuraan decided to stay with aunt Hanim out of respect for her mother. It would not be respectable, I was told, if she enjoyed more sacrality than her mother. After all, her mother had contributed a significant percentage to the cost of her journey. There are many would be pilgrims back home who postpone their pilgrimage because their parents had not yet been. It was disrespectful to your parents to perform the Hajj if they had not yet done so. Nuraan's decision not to climb Mount Hira had something to do with this respect. We all rationalize our actions. We understood.

As Shireen and I started our long climb to the top we witnessed a Wahabi sign that discouraged pilgrims from embarking on this climb. I was convinced that if they had it all their way, we would not have been allowed to visit the cave. They are against the veneration of stone. They are less inclined to venerate the dead. They are less inclined to worship the dead. They would like to impose their will on us. We decided to climb.

The walk to the top was not easy. Shireen and I stopped at least twice to catch our breath and savour some zamzam water that we had brought along with us. We were infused with holiness. We were infused with the charisma of Hajar and Ishmael. Along the way we passed a number of older citizens committed to do the trek to the top. There were older men and women who stopped for extended periods along the way. They must have been people of immense faith. Or maybe of those who had to return home with the charisma that the cave was to routinize. Their Hajj would be admired even more by their friends if they returned with the story of the cave. People would marvel at their courage to have climbed the famous mountain. I admired them.

Once we reached the peak I thought it was all accomplished. The toughest part was still to come. It was clear that Shireen would not be able to climb the steep descent to the cave. She followed me as far as she could. With the cave in sight and still about five metres left to the entrance, Shireen decided to err on the side of caution. She would leave the last lap to me. I slid down the treacherous decline and reached the mouth of the cave to be met by a visitor as zealous as I waiting in turn to enter the cave. I had come this far. I had to sit inside the space where the angel Gabriel had pressed the prophet's chest. It was hard for me to contain my excitement. I called out aloud to Shireen that I was next.

Once inside I decided to take my time in savouring history. I immediately performed the same prayer as we Muslims do when we enter a mosque for the first time. The cave was barely big enough to accommodate one person. I was alone. The solitude of this space said something about wanting to find gnosis. This type of space is for those who need more than the average person from the God. Mohammad, the prophet of Islam, had a special meeting here once. The angel Gabriel was sent by the God to give him a revelatory message here. The powerful Gabriel is said to have pressed his chest so hard that eventually the first verses of the Qur'an sprouted forth.

I was always told that the prophet was illiterate. I was always taught that his revelatory messages were miraculous as the God had chosen an illiterate man to reveal the thousands of verses of the Qur'an to. I was told that the holy revelation to an illiterate man was the biggest miracle of the Qur'an. I wondered at the workings of the God. I questioned the decisions of the God. The first word that the prophet uttered at his encounter with the powerful angel Gabriel sent by the God was Iqra' (recite). Three times Gabriel was said to press the prophet's chest in order to illicit a response. After Gabriel's third pressing demand the word Iqra' was said to be uttered by the prophet. Now, recite is very different from read. It all made sense to me as I contemplated this history in the cave. The prophet of Islam lived during a time when a writing and reading culture was in an infancy stage in seventh century Arabia. As a rule, people did not read and write in his society. He could not have been illiterate. Literacy was not defined by being able to read or write. The God did not choose an illiterate agent for his famous text.

The God must have known that the prophet was the most talented kahin (poet) with possibly the best memory in his community. The God chose the most literate man in the entire desert region. My God is all-knowing, my God is most merciful…Allah knows best. The clergy back home will hear of this.

After this insight I returned to my surroundings. I savoured these surroundings. I was not going to venerate the stone around me. I was endeared by the history. I was in awe of the prophet's accomplishments. This was where it all begun. Not even Shireen would have this honour. Maybe the blind mystic helped me slide down these slopes. Maybe he was instructed by the God to do so. Allah knows best…

I could see the admiration on Shireen's face when I came out of the famous hole. For a moment I looked out at the scenery that lay before me. I then realised how high this mountain was. From that spot I viewed the expanse of Saudi Arabia. From that point this mountain seemed higher that Table Mountain. From that point there was nothing else to think about than who I was. From that point I realised how small I was. The voice of the blind mystic echoed clearly, "You are a nothing, don't think you are special, you are only the instrument of Allah". After settling with this thought the blind man's voice echoed again, "which is it of the mercy of your Lord that you deny". I was shaking at the thought of how small I was in this enormous universe. I felt cold and my body was shaking. I barely made it to the top of the mountain where Shireen reached out her hand to pull me over the last incline. I shared my experience with her. I share my experience with you. There are certain things in life that only words can explain. Few of us have the luxury to enjoy this sight. There are many old people here. Many of us invite the eschaton at an old age. How lucky Shireen. I learnt at an early age that a good young person is worth more than a good old person. I learnt at an early age that a lifetime of goodness outweighs the gaining of goodness at an advanced age.

There are many old people here.

Our aged friends were waiting patiently for our return at the foot of the mountain. They did not enquire about our experiences at the cave. I could understand their quiet. Life is not always fair. I remembered then that they also serve who serve with patience. My friends, I must add, had lots of patience. I wondered if I would have their abundance of patience if I was so lucky to attain their age.

The carbon smoke of the bus was already filling the surrounds as we embarked. The driver, Pakistani I learnt, was not overly concerned about time. His only duty for the day was to drive us to

Mount Hira and back. The workers here have a very different attitude towards work than those workers that I have met in North America or even South Africa. Time here was regulated by the time for prayer. Everything stops when it comes to the five prayer times during the day. The God rules all schedules. It is both frustrating and refreshing. I enjoyed the fact that even though money was a primary motivator for some, even these individuals could not overrule the limitations set by the God. I was frustrated by the laidback attitude that some adopted by always answering, "if the God wills, it will happen". For these individuals it is always "if the God wills". It can sometimes be equated to the Spanish and South American cultural mañana (tomorrow). There is nothing here that is so urgent that it cannot wait until tomorrow, except for the salat. The secular nations can learn something from this society. These people still have time for daytime siestas. These people still have time for the God. These people still have magic. I pray to Allah that the day doesn't come when this society has to say goodbye to magic.

The afternoon was spent doing Shireen's favourite pastime: window shopping. The prices are not set here. We as shoppers were allowed to negotiate a better price for the commodities, many of which were very obviously produced by the same manufacturers. The prices varied depending on the mood of the sales person or whether Shireen or I were doing the negotiations. I was playing along as always, silently wishing for the call to prayer to end my ordeal. The God is merciful I thought when the call eventually came.

After the late afternoon prayer Shireen and I decided to treat ourselves to a meal at one of the many inexpensive restaurants in our street. We had cooked for ourselves from the time we arrived. Shireen's frugality and thrift in wanting to cook for us was appreciated when our weak currency had to be converted to the strong US dollar or the Saudi riyal in order to purchase daily rations for our stay in Makkah. Her Protestant-like ethic had another motivation. She wanted to save on food so that she could have extra cash for gifts to take home. Tonight was different. I was going to pay for the meal from my small personal allowance. Shireen seemed excited at this proposition.

The restaurant that we chose was packed. We had navigated our journey through a string of these small restaurants before deciding on this one. The in and out shuffling of hordes of customers attracted us. We were hoping to find a good meal at a reasonable price. This was a South Asian restaurant, Pakistani, Bangladeshi or Indian. We could not tell. The smell of the curries was mouth-watering. I was excited. We ordered naans, lamb curry and a breyani with samoosas and papadams for starters. It was all delectable and fresh and in the end cost only a couple of US dollars. We had discovered that eating at these restaurants was so reasonable that Shireen and her frugality decided to treat us the following night. We were going to make a habit of this. Before I forget, the mango juice here must have been the best in the world.

Our friends back at the hotel were quite amused at our culinary discoveries. They could not understand our excitement. Only later did we discover that almost every one of these restaurants was manned by south Asian cooks. It was very difficult to find anything on these streets but south Asian cuisine with the odd Turkish restaurant and the occasional camel shwarma. We might as well have been in London or Delhi, the food was mostly south Asian. This said, the following morning Boeta Mustapha treated me to a goat's head stew with naan bread at a breakfast dive only a few meters from our hotel. I was experiencing Hajj. I was excited to savour more. What did the God have in store for us next? Allah is merciful…Allah is all-knowing…Allah knows best.

Chapter 7: The Heifer

> *"Thalika alkitabu la rayba feehi hudan lilmuttaqeen"*
> [This is the Book about which there is no doubt,
> a guidance for those conscious of Allah]

It is an obligation in Islamic law to offer a goat, sheep, cow or camel in sacrifice before the journey of the Hajj proper begins in Makkah. Abraham was requested by the God to slaughter his son Ishmael as a sign of his faith to the God. In his mercy, the God substituted a ram for the young Ishmael. This Hajj ritual of animal sacrifice finds its roots in this story. All pilgrims, who can afford to do so, have to find an agent who can buy them an animal for sacrifice before the physical journey of the Hajj can commence. Shireen and I were offered an opportunity to visit the grand market some fifteen kilometers from Makkah to view our potential sacrifices.

We were solicited by a number of slaughter agents to part with our money for the convenience of having them choose and slaughter an animal for us before we left for the market. The sales techniques of these good folk could compare with the best in the world. A successful agent could collect upwards of a hundred stipends from trusting pilgrims. We were described the fattest lambs in the world. We were sold the tallest camels in the world. We were promised the cheapest rams in the world. We decided to see these sacrifices for ourselves.

The market place was demarcated by a few thousand pens of a variety of animals surrounded by a few million square kilometers of desert sand. There were no extraordinary sized animals. Most of the animals seemed as if they were fed just enough to make it over the next few days before the big slaughter. We enquired what our stipulated stipend would buy. Remember, we had to buy two animals, one for Shireen and one for me. You can just imagine the shock on our faces when we saw what our supposed stipend, set by the agents from back home, would buy. A miniature goat was all our three hundred Saudi riyals could purchase. Even Shireen's frugality couldn't accept the offering that we were to make in order to satisfy the God. In the end, we paid twice the set price for a couple of average looking goats. I was convinced the God would not have been happy with a miniature goat to represent the famous Ishmael. I was convinced that those agents would not have cared. Money can buy anything here. I had learnt at an early age that money can even buy perception.

Satisfied with our purchases we made our way back to the city of the God. The sun was merciless. We were happy to be greeted by Boeta Mustapha in the foyer of the hotel without air-conditioning. At least we would be able to have a shower before the next ritual.

We were leaving the hotel for the late afternoon prayer when Boeta Mustapha introduced us to one of his famous Sheikh friends whom he had met earlier that day. The good-looking Sheikh, Achmat Amieroodien from Cape Town, was excited because he had been invited to meet with the Saudi High Commissioner for Hajj and his delegation. The Sheikh would be one of a number of South Africans given this invitation. I was jealous that

I did not carry such an office. How I longed to sit in such a meeting. How I longed to witness sacred negotiations. My jealousy was short-lived as the Sheikh turned to me and offered to take me along. I wasn't sure if it was Shireen's beauty that fuelled the invitation as the Sheikh's gaze never once shifted from Shireen even while he was in conversation with me. I wasn't going to let further jealousy bother me. I said yes immediately. In response, Sheikh Achmat Amieroodien offered to take Shireen and me out for dinner after the meeting, which according to him, would last no longer than ten to twenty minutes.

The meeting was held in a five-star hotel located one hundred and eighty degrees from our sleeping quarters. These people have money, was my first thought. No expense was spared. The finger meal and drinks were of the highest quality.

These Saudi tour moguls and government officials knew how to lay out a spread. The leadership on the stage at the front of this plush hall had to be Saudi nationals. Their red chequered scarves with the sharp pointed fronts were a dead giveaway. There were Sheikhs and travel agents from all corners of the earth. Even the scoundrel tour agent from Cape Town who had swindled aunty Hanim's life savings was present.

The meeting was started with a reading from the God's holy Qur'an. I wasn't surprised; the reading was led by a Wahabi Sheikh. How else? This was their domain. We were on their turf. They owned the keys to the Kabah. They owned the rights to the last pillar in Islam. I had learnt at an early age that he who owns power, owns the right to impose his will. I had learnt at an early age that power has three dimensions: you need money, culture and politics in order to own power. I learnt that day that the Saudi Wahabis had power. I learnt on that day that the Wahabis were imposing their will.

The meeting continued in Arabic with no translations into other languages. The fact that less than ten percent of the Muslim world understands Arabic did not matter. The Wahabi culture is embedded in that language. The tone of the speaker's voice was one of reprimand. The tone was of admonishment. The speaker's demeanour was like that of a criminal judge delivering sentence. The manner of the speaker was like one who shows disgust of another. Only when he had completed his tirade did another red chequered scarf translate his final sentences. In judge-like style he said, "If you South African travel agents continue one more year with your deception, fraud and lies, we will not issue you or your people another visa to come on Hajj." The room was silent. Sheikh Achmat Amieroodien's face turned the same colour as the lily white cloak that hung so handsomely on his body. I turned quickly to see if I could catch a glimpse of aunty Hanim's predator. This fraudster tried to hide his face behind one of his henchmen that he had brought along for the free meal.

We left the building with our tails between our legs. Sheikh Achmat Amieroodien made some excuse about having forgotten about a meeting that he had arranged for the evening. Shireen was not going to have dinner with the suave Sheikh. I was happy not to dine with deceit. I had learnt at an early age not to trust the man who portrays sacrality. I had learnt at an early age to be wary of the man who rationalizes all actions through the holy book. I had learnt at an early age to not equate good looks with goodness. I had learnt at an early age that the priest has to compromise his ethics sometimes. I had learnt at an early age that the priest and the politician were similar.

There was some disappointment in Shireen's face when I told her that the dinner had been called off. I offered to take her to a different Pakistani restaurant rather than our favourite spot. I knew it was no consolation; the Pakistani restaurants all served the same cuisine. It is wonderful how these Pakistani workers impose their culture through cuisine. It is wonderful how the Pakistani workers impose their identity. It is wonderful how a slave fights back against a master. This night I met the Pakistani owner of the restaurant. He was wearing a red chequered scarf with a sharp pointed front. I had learnt at an early age that the slave aspires to take on the identity of the master. I saw a Pakistani slave.

We left the restaurant after a few glasses of mango juice. The image of the Pakistani slave was etched in my memory. As we walked back to the hotel, passing many clothing stores along the way, the smell of the yellow-label tea travelled with us. There were many tea-vendors out tonight. Business must be brisk I thought. At a distance I saw Boeta Mustapha sitting at a tea-vendor's cart with a chubby gentleman having a cuppa. I asked Shireen to excuse me for a couple of minutes so that I could catch up on some man's talk with the fat uncles. Shireen had other plans. She wanted more shopping. It was a good enough compromise: she could do the woman thing while I would talk about the big things in the world with my nascent friends. I had learnt at an early age that men talk about the big things in life, world politics, sport and religion. I had learnt at an early age that women talk about the little things in life, like the children's schooling and the rent. I was looking forward to some serious conversation.

It turned out that Boeta Mustapha's friend was his brother, Arabi. My new acquaintance was an Imam from a small town outside the Cape. Arabi was the pet-name Boeta Mustapha used for his older brother. Imam Arabi had a dark stain on his forehead. This stain to the skin appears after years of prostration. During the salat ritual we Muslims place our foreheads on the ground in complete submission to the God. Only years of regular prostration can cause such skin damage. In the Muslim world men are revered for this dark pigmentation. It is one of the only cases that I am aware of where the dark skin pigmentation trumps a white skin tone. Religions are powerful socialising agents; they can even transgress hierarchies and norms of racial constructions. For a moment I thought about how powerful a white man would be with a dark-stained forehead. The contrast in skin colour must add to the sacrality we would bestow on him.

Imam Arabi was friendly and easy going. I could tell that he was different from some of the other clerics I knew from my city. He was less concerned about material things. He was a simple man. He had to be a teacher of the faith. He was constantly teaching. He did not ask questions about who I was or if I knew anything of the Islamic teachings that spewed forth throughout the conversation. I was a stranger to him yet he told me personal things about his experiences in Makkah. I had learnt at an early age that we are inclined to tell strangers more than we would tell our best friends. I had learnt early in my life to listen carefully to the stranger for the stranger could become my friend. I listened intently to Imam Arabi. Imam Arabi became my friend.

My new friend had visited Makkah twenty seven years in succession. His entire life must evolve around the Hajj I thought. How happy I was. How excited I was when I thought about how much I could learn from my learned friend. Shireen would be jealous. From here on she would have to share her shopping time with my new-found friend. I had learnt at an early age that a spouse can be jealous of a friend. I had learnt at an early age that a spouse must learn to live with her jealousy. I had learnt at an early age that big talk trumps little talk. I had learnt at an early age that they also serve who serve with patience. Shireen would have to be patient.

Imam Arabi was no ordinary cleric; he was the leader of the Naqshabandi Sufi order in my country. I was intoxicated by this knowledge. I was going to learn secrets of another world through my new friend. I listened to his every word. I watched his every action. I wanted to be like him. The Sufi Imam would meet me after the Morning Prayer at around six the following morning for yellow-label tea and conversation. I could not wait.

As promised Imam Arabi was waiting for me outside the grand mosque. The light was beginning to pierce its way through the darkness. There is something special about rising early. There was something mystical in the air. Shireen was happy to return to our hotel for some further sleep. I was ready for the Sufi. Imam Arabi attracted at least ten dark-skinned women beggars. He handed everyone a Saudi riyal until he protested that he had nothing left. They bought his truth. I wanted to get his take on these beggars. Without asking he answered the question foremost in my mind. "They are also the creations of Allah," was his soft response. And in the next breath came his startling revelation, "Remember you are a nothing, don't think you are special, you are only the instrument of Allah." If I had doubts about the office of my new friend, those doubts left then. I listened even more intently to the Imam. I remained a stranger. He revealed all. Our conversation continued.

Chapter 8: The Narratives of Imam Arabi

"Kaf-Ha-Ya-Ain-Sad"
[There are no translations or understandings to the above]

Imam Arabi learnt to read the Qur'an from memory by the time he was seven. Thereafter he studied the sayings of the prophet and spent the rest of his life studying Islamic texts that his spiritual teachers deemed necessary. He visited the city of Makkah for the first time at the age of forty and had been here performing Hajj for twenty seven consecutive years. It was during his first visitation that he had heard the voice of the prophet Muhammad. He was standing besides the tomb of the prophet, in the mosque of the prophet in Medina, doing the ritual greeting of the prophet's grave when it happened. The prophet answered his greeting with,"and peace also with you". He said that he could still vividly hear the voice of the prophet in his mind today. I was fascinated by his story and wanted the learned Imam to continue the conversation but Imam Arabi needed to hand some riyals to beggars who were waiting patiently to catch his eye. Before he continued with his experiences he quickly remarked that you never know who these beggars were. Sometimes there are holy people of the past that are sent by the God to test us, he continued. He said that he had never refused to give money or food to a beggar in his entire life. These beggars took priority over our conversation. I was patient, I wanted to hear more.

It was obvious that the Imam wanted to spend time with me. I was wondering why this would be. This cleric did not need me to bestow sacred power on him. I had learnt at an early age that we the laity bestow power on the clerics. I had leant at an early age that clerics are driven by this power. It was clear that Imam Arabi was not in search of that power.

The chubby cleric had a healthy appetite and a sweet tooth. We ate our breakfast within minutes. I was trying to keep up with the Imam. Normally I would eat more slowly and savour the yellow-label tea. Today it was all about getting breakfast out of the way for the more important conversation.

As people passed us many would stop to greet the Imam. They must have been from South Africa. The Imam was well known. After a while Imam Arabi informed me that he teaches Hajj classes at his home and has in excess of six hundred students per year. These students pay a few rands extra every year to have him, their spiritual leader, accompany them on their holy pilgrimage. This explained the twenty seven consecutive years of pilgrimage that the Imam performed.

The Imam explained to me that it was easy for me to enter the world of the chosen few. He would perform a special prayer and invite me into the group. I would form part of a chain with the God. There were a few things I had to know before he could proceed with his initiation ceremony. First, that I had to be humane to all of God's people on earth, be they Muslim or non-Muslim. Second, that I would not be able to be unjust or unethical as the God and those other members along the chain would shake the chain vehemently to rid the system of the wrong-doer. Third, that if I was to wrong, the God would punish me immediately.

Fourth, if I performed good deeds, showed grace and respect for the God's creations, including the environment, I would achieve the ultimate gifts from the God: peace and the ability to discern the workings of the God in mundane action. For a while I thought about this small return, peace, in compensation for a lifetime's commitment to all that is good. Peace? I then remembered. This was the goal of most great religious traditions. For example, the Buddhists' first noble truth states,"Life is suffering". This is followed by the second Buddhist noble truth,"Suffering is caused by desire". Peace began to make more sense to me. A state of peace would take away any unnecessary desires and life would not be one of want and suffering. Life may even end up being blissful. The God offered his ultimate reward. Material without peace was valueless. Poverty lost its meaning if a state of ultimate peace could be attained. I opted for the latter.

Imam Arabi did not waste any time. He started his prayer with:"I, the God, and my angels bring salutations on the prophet Muhammad. O you people who believe, join me in bringing peace and salutations on the prophet of Islam. Allah brings peace and blessings on the prophet Muhammad."He explained that there were four components to this chain: the God, the angels, the prophet Muhammad and the believing humans. I was now part of this chain. It was as easy as that. I felt special. I had made the commitment. I had to watch my step from here.

All I had to do was to invoke this prayer whenever I was in need and answers would be presented. For me it was twice lucky. First it was the journey in the mosque of the prophet, now the Naqshabandi Sufi's invitation. There was something that struck me as odd. I was going to see the workings of the God in ordinary human behaviour and action. I was going to interpret human action and see divine workings in it. It wasn't too far away from the philosophy that I had learnt in Islam. In the creation story in Islam, the God creates humankind out of dust. Once the lifeless physical being is built, the God blows his spirit into the structure in order to give it life. We all carried the soul of the God. More importantly, all humans carried the spirit of the God in them, even the Christians, the Jews and the Atheists. Even a black person walked around with the spirit of the God in him. The God did not discriminate. The God's spirit in me would not be able to discriminate. I, Sheikh Kimal Baig, would never again be able to discriminate against any of the God's creation. His chain would shake vehemently I was warned.

These new insights would make me view the world and the behaviour of its human occupants more carefully in the future. If the God did not discriminate, certainly my God didn't, I was convinced, then He could even use non-Muslims as instruments to carry through his will. All humans carry his ruh (spirit). I had to rethink any negotiations with the Kufar (non-believers) in future dealings, at minimum they were infused with the same essence as me. I had learnt at an early age that we humans are born with empty slates. Unlike the lion cub, we do not have the capacity to deal with adult life at an early age. We need to learn a communication system, including a language. We needed to learn a specific culture which itself underwent change. We even have to learn the religion of our forefathers and our society in order to conform and behave correctly. I had learnt at an early age that we humans are products of a socializing process. The idea that the God created us all as equals, no matter what colour or creed, was appealing to me. I was going to tell Shireen about this. The clerics back home will hear about this.

Wow! I thought, as I played gymnastics with the new ideas in my brain, and please don't think it's that little guy Satan playing with my mind. I had long ago been able to keep our discussions private. The real Sufi is he or she who is able to see the workings of the divine in mundane action. We were all cogs in the God's great enterprise and He activates who He wills in order to achieve whatever He, the great metaphysic, wants. These cogs consist of all of humankind, Christian, Muslim, Jew, Hindu, Atheist, fence-sitter…it did not matter. The God used us all. We are his creations to be used. Of course all this made sense when I used my monotheistic lens.

Now I wasn't able to engage people of other religions here as only Muslims are allowed to enter the city of Makkah. Approximately twenty kilometers from the city, on the main highway, was a huge road sign in both Arabic and English which read, "No non-Muslims may enter Makkah". My first thoughts were about the history of this famous city and its inhabitants. Before the coming of Islam this city had been the business hub of the region. Traders from all over the region, including the Byzantine and the Sassanian world came to ply their wares here. The prophet of Islam himself engaged Jews, Christians, Pagans and Sabbeans in Makkah during the first thirteen years of his tenure as a prophet. The

Kabah itself housed the pagan gods, al-lat, al-manat and al-uza. At a certain time in Islamic history the decision must have been made to keep non-Muslims out. I had learnt at an early age that religions become extremely powerful when they have state support. I had learnt at an early age that religions grow significantly when they receive state support. I was convinced the growth of Islam in many parts of the world was a product of state support. Makkah had state support.

Imam Arabi and I parted ways as he had other students to engage. Besides, Shireen would be most upset if my new friend was to occupy all of her shopping time. Shireen was waiting anxiously in our hotel room for my return. She did not even enquire about the teachings of the master. She wanted to visit a new shopping area today. We decided to make our way to the fancy part of the town where the posh pilgrims stayed. The west side of the city housed hotels called the Hilton, the Arabella, the Marriot, the Sheraton, and the Ritz Plaza. I wondered if the fancy hotels in North America and Europe, with these very names, had interest in these five-star mega hotels towering over the grand mosque. I was certain that some of the rooms had a bird's eye view of the Kabah and all that happens there. If I was so lucky to have a room there I would be able to do my Leutesehen while sipping my yellow-label tea without having to leave my bed. I heard the little monster whisper in my brain, if wishes were horses, beggars would ride. I left that thought right there.

Shireen was excited about the trip to these up-market shopping malls. The food court caught my attention first. McDonald's,

Kentucky, Starbucks, Subway Sandwiches…they were all here. It was as if I had entered a mall in New York or Toronto. I suddenly felt the urge to savour a Big Mac. The line-up was long, but as was the case in other cities where McDonald's sell their cuisine, every sixty seconds a customer was happy to move along with their burgers. Shireen was happy to settle for a Big Mac Meal, supersized, but complained about the price as she compared it to the cost of a curry meal in the east end where we stayed. True to form, McDonald's delivered a burger equal to any we had had in South Africa or North America. I wondered whether the Arab franchise holders of these big name global chains had to kowtow to the American bosses. I wondered whether these Arab bosses aspired to be slaves.

After lunch we spent a few hours at the Marriot hotel. It was indeed an American investment and had all the trimmings of its American counterpart. Non-Muslims were not allowed to enter the city of Makkah as the billboard clearly stated. I was wondering whether these non-Muslim shareholders could watch the circumambulations at the Kabah when they visit their investments. These hotels certainly had the best locations in the city of Makkah and its shareholders were guaranteed full occupation during the expensive Hajj season. Yes, I know I said it before, but I have to say it again, money can buy anything here.

There were no beggars in this neck of the woods. These posh pilgrims are denied that luxury. Imam Arabi would not be at home here. He would not be as needed as in the east end where we lived. There are no tea-vendors here. There are no strings of

Pakistani restaurants here. Many of these posh pilgrims never venture to our side of the world. I began to wonder about the individual experiences of Hajj. It can be so different for the rich and so rich for the poor. I had learnt at an early age that the poor are more religious than the wealthy. I had learnt at an early age that the poor need the God more than the wealthy. I was wondering whether the God needs the poor. I was wondering whether there would be a God without the poor.

Shireen and I walked back to our hotel without the air-conditioning. We did not belong at the Marriot. We missed the heat of our one-star dive. We missed the smell of the yellow-label tea. We missed the beggars that swarmed around us like flies around a dead fish. We longed to be back in our neighbourhood where the God rules all. We walked as fast as we could to all that we longed for. I cannot explain this feeling…Allah knows best.

Chapter 9: The Kiswah

"Said the Prophet…"

Our group decided to visit the factory that manufactures the Kiswah1 the following day. The history of the manufacture of this covering is both polemical and interesting. It is not certain whether Ismael, son of Abraham, or the great- great grandfather of the prophet, Adnan bin Ad, had first started the tradition of draping the Kabah in a black cloth. What is certain is that it is a tradition that pre- dates Islam.

The Saudi government had built this factory specifically to manufacture the Kiswah. We were told that approximately two hundred people worked here. The cloth is made of natural silk imported from various parts of the world. Verses of the Qur'an are embroided on the cloth with gilded silver wire threads. No expense is spared in the manufacture and all processes are done on the premises. The workers were friendly and quite willing to show us around even allowing us to physically thread some of the embroidery.

A replica of the Kabah was also on display. Tourists could get a feel the cloth and enter a make-shift Kabah to get the feel of being inside the real building: of course entry was only allowed the King and his cohort of disciples from the family of the Quiraish tribe. I accepted that this would be as close as it gets. I accepted that this was part of the constructed realities of Wahabi Islam. Maybe in time the rules will change, yet again. Allah knows best…

On our departure I met an Islamic scholar from Germany. He was your typical teacher. I could ask him questions, I thought. He would be willing to entertain me. I had learnt at an early stage in my life that all of life is a stage. I had learnt at an early stage in my life that the props and circumstances change. I had learnt at an early age that we are all actors on a stage and we play the role that the circumstances demand. I had learnt at an early age that our roles as actors cut across cultures. I was waiting to engage my German teacher…

Chapter 10:
The Memory of Sheikh Mahmood Vaybier

> *"No summer's bloom. A polar night of icy harshness and darkness awaits us, no matter who triumphs now"*

I greeted the learned Sheikh with the ritual greeting of As-sa-laamu-alaikum. His response was automatic: wa-alaikum-al-sa-laam. It was as if he had anticipated my contact. I sensed sadness in his eyes. Despite the sadness the teacher in him was hungry to engage a student. I was a willing student. In this environment I had to change my role as an ever-questioning critical student to the role of an unquestioning student that my Muslim world demands. I was to listen to truth and faith statements as all that would pour forth would be supported by the Qur'an. There is no room for critical thinking here as the ontology is firmly supported by the episteme of the God. However, the conversation that continued was beyond my expectations.

Sheikh Vaybier's Arabic was perfect. His English was limited. We decided to continue in German. I complained to him that it seemed to me that the Wahabis, the Sunnis and the Shi'i were disputing events in history. It was as if they were venerating history and were willing to maintain sectarian divide based on history. In the end, it was about worshipping history. I asked his opinion on the matter. If you have the time, I will explain it all, he said. That is, if you have the time he courteously continued. Of course I have the time, was my amiable response.

Let me paint the structures of Islam first, and then maybe you will be able to decide for yourself what orthodoxy and orthopraxy means in Sunni, Shi'i or Wahabi versions of Islam, he continued. I quickly enquired what version of Islam interested him. Instantly he replied,"I follow the version that is available on the day". This was interesting I thought as I figuratively rubbed my hands together in anticipation. I was virtually drooling with my eyes fixed on this heretic.

Islam is a Near Eastern monotheistic tradition in which Old Testament, Jewish and Christian elements are evident, the Sheikh insisted. Very early on in the development of Islam incorporated certain Jewish rituals but soon morphed into a religion very different from Judaism. The Sheikh pointed out that the prophet of Islam had asked his early followers to fast with the Jews over Yomkipur and that the early believers faced Jerusalem for the first couple of years before they were asked by the prophet to change direction and face Makka during the prayer rituals. During the initial phase of Islam the tradition developed within the busy commercial centre of Makka but since the prophet had difficulties in convincing the elites about his religious messages the prophet Muhammad had to withdraw from the Makkan world and its commercial orientations. At this juncture all my attention was focused on the Sheikh's lecture. In Medina, the Sheikh continued, the religion transformed from its pure form into a national Arabic warrior religion and later into a religion with strong emphasis on status. Think about the early followers of Islam, like Abu-Bakr and Umar, who helped make the religion of the prophet successful. These men were all members of powerful families. And for the next couple of hundred years Islam's religious elites were all members of political elites.

The early Muslims in their jihad (holy wars) were not fighting to necessarily convert people. Rather, the main purpose of war was to subjugate the 'people of the book' to humbly pay the taxes and tributes due to the Muslim army. This method assured Islam growth to the top of this world's social scale. Yes, the Muslim Sheikh insisted, the goal was to gain as much material from other religions. Islam, he continued, is the religion of masters during the early centuries. Spoils of war are important in its decrees, in the promises, and above all in the expectations characterizing especially the early period of the religion. The ultimate elements of its economic ethic were purely feudal. The most pious adherents of the religion in its first generation became the wealthiest, or more correctly, enriched themselves with military booty – in the widest sense – more than did other members of the faith. The Sheikh was bordering on profanity, I thought. His historical knowledge was sound. I struggled to find challenges to the Sheikh's scathing analyses at this point and decided to let him continue with his diatribe.

The role played by amassing wealth due to spoils of war and from political enlargement in Islam stands directly opposite to the role played by wealth in the Puritan religion. The Muslim tradition proudly shows off, with pleasure, the perfumes, luxuries and beard-coiffure of the pious. The saying that "When God blesses a man with prosperity he likes to see the signs thereof visible upon him" – made by the Prophet, according to tradition (hadith), to the rich who appeared before him in ragged attire – stands directly opposite to the Protestant economic ethic and fits well with feudal conceptions of status. The Sheikh continued. This saying would mean, in our language, that a wealthy man is obligated "to live in keeping with his status." In the Qur'an, the Prophet is represented as completely rejecting every type of monasticism (rahbaniya), though not all asceticism.

Remember, continued the Sheikh, the Prophet did accord respect to fasting, begging and indignities suffered by those in captivity. The Prophet's attitude in opposition to chastity may have sprung from personal motivations, the Sheikh insisted.

The learned Sheikh Vaybier had to take a zamzam break before he could continue. I enquired about his sleeping patterns without thinking this to be out of place. He unhesitatingly responded that he had trouble sleeping at night. I quickly followed up with a battery of questions, while I helped myself to the wonderful zamzam. How is your appetite, do you suffer any stomach problems, and very slowly I added…any sexual problems? The Sheikh did not even blink and responded with certainty, "I suffer all of those". I was convinced then that what I had thought was sadness in his eyes was in fact depression.

The Sheikh continued: but Islam was never really a religion of salvation; the ethical concept of salvation was actually alien to Islam. Allah was a lord of unlimited power, although merciful, the fulfillment of whose commandments was not beyond human power. An essentially political character marked all the chief ordinances of Islam: stopping private Bedouin battles in the interest of increasing the group's striking power against external foes; limitations on illegitimate forms of sexual behaviour and the regulation of legitimate sexual relations along strongly patriarchal lines; the prohibition of usury; prescription of taxes for war; and the injunction to support the poor. Equally political in character is the distinctive religious obligation in Islam, its only required dogma: the recognition of Allah as the one god and of Muhammad as his prophet. In addition, there were the obligations to journey to Makkah once during a lifetime, to fast by day during the month of Ramadan, to attend services once a week, and to observe the obligation of daily prayers. Finally, Islam imposed such requirements for everyday living as the wearing of distinctive clothing and the avoidance of certain unclean foods, of wine, and of gambling. The restrictions against gambling obviously had important consequences for the religion's attitude toward speculative business enterprises.

The Sheikh's knowledge of early Islam was notable. He continued: There was nothing in ancient Islam like an individual quest for salvation, nor was there any mysticism. The religious promises in the earliest period of Islam pertained to this world. Wealth, power and glory were all military promises, and even the world beyond is pictured in Islam as a soldier's sensual paradise. The Sheikh had a way of getting to the root of the ideas that underpinned the religion. He must have spent many years analyzing Islam, I thought. The learned Sheikh continued: the depiction of the prophet of Islam as being free of sin is a late theological construction. This is scarcely consistent with the actual nature of the Prophet's strong sensual passions and his explosions of wrath over every small provocation. Such a picture is strange even to the Qur'an. The original feudal idea of sin remained dominant in orthodox Islam, for which sin is a composite of ritual impurity, ritual sacrilege (shirk, i.e., polytheism), and disobedience to what the prophet said. Islam also displays other characteristics of a distinctively feudal spirit: the obviously unquestioned acceptance of slavery, serfdom and polygamy; subjugation of women; the essentially ritualistic character of religious obligations; and finally, the great simplicity of religious requirements and the even greater simplicity of the modest ethical requirements.

Islam was not brought any closer to Judaism and to Christianity in decisive matters by such developments as the formation of the order of dervishes (still today strongly under Indian influence). Judaism and Christianity were specifically bourgeois-urban religions, whereas for Islam the city had only political importance. The petty-bourgeois stratum was largely the carrier of the dervish religion, which was disseminated practically everywhere and gradually grew in power, finally surpassing the official ecclesiastical religion. This type of religion, with its mystical elements, with its essentially irrational and extraordinary character, and with its official and thoroughly traditionalistic ethic of everyday life, became influential in Islam's missionary enterprise because of its great simplicity. It directed the conduct of life into paths whose effect was plainly opposite to the methodical control of life found among Puritans. In other words, the Sheikh continued, the mystical forms of Islam including the dervishes moved the religion of Islam away from a religion that could and did in fact have an orientation toward capital accrual and financial esteem. Wow, I thought, this Sheikh was in fact saying that Islam can never be a world economic superpower as long as it ascribes to mystical forms. I wondered what the Sheikhs back home would say about this. I wondered if these thoughts ever crossed their minds.

I could see that the Sheikh was growing tired. He continued nevertheless. The ideal personality type in the religion of Islam was not the scholarly scribe, but the warrior. I had always thought of the Muslim as the scholar. But then I remembered that the first few centuries of Islam were defined by military episodes and that the scholars were often imprisoned, like Ibn Hanbal for example. Then there is also the late entry of philosophy to the religion. I remembered, it was almost five hundred years after the death of the Prophet that the great systematiser, al-Ghazali, marries philosophy and mysticism to theology in Islam. Yes, the Sheikh had a point, I thought.

To be sure, there were ascetic sects among Muslims, the Sheikh continued. Large groups of ancient Islamic warriors were characterized by a trend toward simplicity; this prompted them from the outset to oppose the rule of the Umayyads. The Umayyads' merry enjoyment of the world presented the strongest contrast to the rigid discipline of the encampment fortresses in which Umar had concentrated Islamic warriors in the conquered domains; in this environment there now arose a feudal aristocracy. But this was the asceticism of a military caste, of a martial order of knights, not of monks. Certainly it was not a middle- class ascetic systemization of the conduct of life. Moreover, it was effective only periodically, and even then it tended to merge into fatalism. Islam was diverted completely from any really methodical control of life by the advent of the cult of saints, and finally by magic.

Sheikh Vaybier was exhausted after his lengthy lecture. I felt as depressed as the Sheikh at the thought of the Sunnis and Shi'i arguing about whose leadership was more legitimate. I felt a depressive wave come over me as I thought about the clerics back home who sold me on the idea that they practiced a form of Islam that is primarily based on the Qur'an and the Sunna (teachings of the prophet). I felt angst at the thought of being led to believe that only certain events in history were sacred. I knew now what caused the Sheikh's depression. I felt the same.

I had many new questions now. How can Islam ever be an economic superpower in modern capitalist environments when the founding ideas negate notions of saving and thrift? I knew now why the Wahabi elites own seven star hotels and palaces that all the production of marble in Italy calls for. Wahabism lies closest to the warrior ideology of the founding father of Islam: its ideological basis is rooted in the first generation of Islam only. Its veneration of history does not exceed the epoch of the second generation of Islamic history. Wahabism is a this-worldly oriented religion. I now know why the dead are buried within hours of their last breath. They worship this world. Their notion of the afterlife, in accordance with the philosophy of the generation of the Prophet, has a limited development of an eschaton. The Sheikh reminded me that the Qur'an attests to this.

I now know why the Ottoman Sunnis lost power for the Islamic world against the growth of modern capitalism. Their leaders aspired to renunciation of this world through twirling, magic and the cult of saints while western capitalist countries built weaponry along rational means including their mastery of modern bureaucracies. For the Sunnis it became a matter of salvation in an afterlife. The extension of this world into an afterlife grew increasingly more important for them as philosophy, mysticism and theology became intertwined. They kept their eyes on the history of the past while the present was snatched away by a more efficient enemy looking at the present and the future.

I now know why the Shi'i worship the Imams. I now know why they venerate the dead. They are waiting for the dead, the Mahdi, to return in order to alleviate their burdens. They self-flagellate in memory of the dead. They are increasingly less concerned with a this-worldly oriented religion. They will have to wait a million culpas before they enjoy the glory of their Sassanian forefathers, I thought.

I asked Sheikh Vaybier where he had attained his knowledge and insights. He shyly answered that this narrative was an attempt at memorizing the works of his German ancestor Maximillian Weber. Like the students who memorize the thirty chapters of the Qur'an, he had tried to memorize the great Maximillian Weber's sociology of Islam from Wirtshaft und Geselschaft Volume II. I walked away from the heretic. I could not offer a line of argument against the learned Sheikh. I felt depressed because of his truth. I needed the God to protect me against the wizardry of the Sheikh's ancestor's intellect. I needed Shireen's faith. I was happy that she did not understand German. Then I remembered I had my experiences; Sheikh Vaybier's forefather could never take that away from me. I had my magic. I needed to escape the depression. I asked Allah for his mercy. This heretic had almost snatched my magic.

Chapter 11: The Teachings of the Urdu Cleric

That evening after my lectures with Sheikh Mahmood Vaybier I struggled to fall asleep. I arose during the night and I was awake before the Morning Prayer not being able to find peace. I blamed it on the German Sheikh. I decided to forget about his teachings as his voice continued to echo in my head. I asked Allah to make the Sheikh's messages go away.

After breakfast that morning an Urdu cleric was giving a lecture in the grand mosque. My Urdu was poor. I asked a friend to translate for me. I trusted my friend's translation. I was certain he would not tell half-truths in translation.

The Urdu cleric started his lecture in a very humble manner but soon turned his demeanor into a tele-evangelic style as his audience grew to thousands. His charisma was unmatched in this neck of the woods. I learnt early in my stay in Makkah that the language of Islam is not only Arabic, but also Urdu, Farsi, Turkish and Indonesian. On many occasions I wished I had the luxury of all these languages. How can we know a people without knowing their languages, let alone the nuances of their languages? Maybe I can waiver from my story for a while and tell you about a book I bought in Makkah entitled Ar-Raheeq Al-Makhtum (The Sealed Nectar) by the author Saifur Rahman al-Mubarakpuri. This book won first prize in a competition set by the Saudi government. The authors had to present a researched essay on the life of the prophet of Islam. One hundred and seventy one entrants were received. The first four prizes went to Urdu texts, the fifth prize to a Hausa text (Nigerian language) and an Arabic text taking sixth place. I was taken aback by this outcome. But after some thought I realized that the Arabic-speaking world is significantly smaller than the Urdu or Indonesian Muslim world. I had heard that Indonesia houses 245 million Muslims, making them by far the biggest Muslim community in the world. In India, Pakistan and Bangladesh combined there must be in excess of 450 million Muslims. The Arab world combined is not even a tenth of the Asian Muslim population. I turned my thoughts back to the Urdu cleric with respect when I thought about the orders of magnitude in the world of Islam. I had gained an open-mindedness to engage the thoughts of an Urdu intellect.

My friend was fast in translation. The Urdu cleric was succinct. There are a few of his thoughts that I would like to share with you. Rather, a few of the translations that my friend was able to relay to me. The Sheikh started: The Qur'an is not about Allah even though the name of Allah appears more than two thousand five hundred times. The Qur'an is aimed at man. In fact, it calls itself "guidance for mankind" (hudan li'l-naas [2:185]). God is purely functional in the Qur'an. God is the Architect of the universe and man. God judges individually and collectively. God is the sustainer of this enterprise and remains the sole judge in a merciful way.

God knows all there is to know about humankind. The Qur'an states, "We created man and We know what the negative whisperings of his mind are and We are nearer to him than his jugular vein!" (50:16). Allah is infinite, the most merciful, and does not entertain partnerships. The Qur'an attests to this:"And God has said, 'Do not take two gods [for] He is only One" (16:51);"God bears witness that there is no god, but He" (3:18); Say [O Muhammad] if there were other gods besides Him, as these people assert, they would all seek their way to the Lord of the Throne" (17:42). God demands He alone be worshipped. However, the Qur'an is not about God but a divine book to guide humankind.

I was very interested in the Urdu cleric's lecture now. I always thought the Qur'an was about worshipping Allah. I had learnt something. It took me all of my life up until this point to learn a basic "truth" of the Qur'an. My teachers back home will hear about this. My teachers back home made me so terrified of the wrath of God that I was too afraid to ask questions about the purpose of the Qur'an. I wanted to know more as we waited for the cleric to catch his breath.

God created humankind just as He created all creatures. God created Adam (first man) out of baked clay (15:26, 28, 33; 6:2; 7:12 and more). Humankind differs from God's other creatures in a fundamental way in that after God fashioned the human mould, then God "breathed My own spirit" into him (15:29; 38:72; and 32:9).

My mind had to take a moment to digest this. We humans all carry the essence of the God with us, I pondered. I carry the spirit of the God in me. You carry the spirit of the God in you. This was profound, I thought. I thought about how badly I had behaved in the past. I had been jealous, greedy, uncaring, selfish, rude, self- centered, arrogant to mention but a few thoughts of my past recollected behaviours. Did the God that lurks in me allow me to experience all of these feelings and actions while silently enduring the scathe of behaviour, I thought. Maybe we have a dualism in us. I had to find out more. If only I could speak Urdu then I would be able to question the learned Sheikh.

The Sheikh continued: After the God created man there was one amongst the jinn (18:50) who protested against Adam's superior knowledge and disobeyed Allah's command to respect Adam. This jinn became known as Satan. Wow, Satan was born after Adam was my immediate thought. Satan was created with the express purpose to keep humankind off the "straight path". Man and woman face a lifelong struggle against an agent, Satan. This said, Satan fails against the virtuous individuals. The Sheikh continued: Nobody is safe from Satan's temptations, no prophets (22:52; 17:53), not even the Prophet Muhammad (s.a.w) (7:200; 41:36). However, remember, said the Sheikh, each person of true faith and determination can overcome the lures of the devil (15:42; 17:65; 16:99). Those among you who can overcome the devil move toward your true fitra [primordial nature] (30:30), the Sheikh continued.

All individuals belong to a society. Society is important toward an understanding of man's role in it. Would there be a need for religion if there were only one human left on earth, asked the Sheikh. Whenever there are two or more persons in a conversation, Allah enters directly. In other words, the God will constitute the third dimension.

Do you not see that God knows everything in the heavens and the earth? There is no secret cliquing of three but that God is the fourth, nor five but that He is the sixth, nor of less than these or more but that He is with them wherever they be. (58:7)

Even though this verse reflects the conversations about the opponents of Islam at the time (pagans and hypocrites), more immediately it means that God is present when two or more people are in conversation, continued the Sheikh. Remember, warned the Sheikh, Allah is ever watchful, and as far as entire societies are concerned, "He is sitting in a watch tower" (89:14), and "no atom in the heavens or the earth ever escapes His notice" (10:61; 34:3). For a while there I thought about another Sheikh, Karl Marx, who once implied that religion is a form of social control, mostly favouring the bourgeoisie. If the owners of capital can have an ever-present watchful eye over their interests then it would serve their needs most. Those who own wealth benefit most by an ever-watchful God said the little demon in my head. I needed to keep my little demons in check if I was to take in all of what my translator presented. Karl Marx was one of my most vociferous demons. It was easier for me to keep him quiet than the other German Satan of the 19th and 20th century. When it came to religion that guy played gymnastics in my head. Fortunately this day he was tone-deaf to religion. I was just about ready to shut out the little demons when another, Sheikh Mahmood Vaybier, whispered that throughout Islamic history, including its ancient form was dominated by wealthy elites. Karl Marx returned. He whispered, If you want to understand anything in life always ask the question, "who benefits?". I had to stop these little guys now, the Urdu Sheikh was moving in a very different direction with his train of thought, if I was to believe my translator.

The Sheikh continued: Muslims around the world know very little about the Qur'an. Repeating the five pillars of Islam or inheritance laws leaves the Muslims with only a superficial understanding of the Qur'an. Just ask some basic questions about the Qur'an to your friends and you will soon learn that I am speaking the truth, the Sheikh continued. If this is true, I thought, then Sheikh Vaybier's painting of the ideal Muslim as a warrior rather than a scholar must have some truth in it. But let the Sheikh continue, I told myself as I kept the little demon at bay. The Qur'an has no consistent story line, no consistent genre, no one knows the chronological revelation of the verses, no one knows for certain the contexts of revelation and to boot there are also the question of abrogated verses, he continued. Can one then accept a statement taken out of the Qur'an from a cleric who has limited education in the area of Qur'anic exegesis, does not have a command of the Arabic language, owns a limited knowledge of historical Islam, let alone the society within which the Qur'an is revealed? What value does the Qur'an hold for the average Muslim who can offer almost nothing of the Qur'an on examination, continued the Sheikh. No doubt there are many who can read the Qur'an from memory yet offer no more than the beautiful poetry embedded in its text. Are we, fourteen hundred years later, still merely poets? Only this time around poets of a foreign language that we have no knowledge of, the Sheikh continued on in tirade. I felt as if the Sheikh had his gaze fixed on me this time around. I felt as if the Sheikh was speaking directly to me. I had to honestly answer in affirmation to all his challenges. I knew this to be the state of affairs where I came from. I was a warrior not a scholar. I was determined to change my state of jahiliyah (ignorance). I was a jahil. My friends and family were jahil. No, less than jahils, they could not even understand the poetic value of the Qur'an. At least the people of jahiliyah could understand the poetry. May Allah have mercy on our limited inquisitive souls. Allah is most merciful…

I wanted to hear no more. I could not understand the Urdu. I could not understand the Arabic. I was not certain that the translator was accurate. I no longer wanted to be led in ignorance. I asked the God to give me the gift of language. I had learnt at an early stage in my life that religion was about language and symbols. I started having doubts about the value of my forefathers who had taught me the symbols without teaching me the language to interpret them. I needed a reformation. I was convinced that my people needed reformation. I was convinced that my people would not agree. I was convinced that my forefathers were stronger than me. I asked the God to silence my forefathers if Islam was to grow to become a superpower once more. The little demon in me quickly answered…Allah knows best.

I had to silence these demons; the 9th of Thul-Hijjah was fast approaching. Shireen and I would soon be on Mount Arafat, Muzdalifah and Mina. I could not afford to have the little monsters whisper their "truths". I walked away in a state of angst and depression to my air-conditionless hotel. I was not going to tell Shireen about my encounter with the Urdu cleric. I was not going to challenge her magic.

Chapter 12: The Plains of Mount Arafat

> *"This day I have perfected for you your religion*
> *and completed My favor upon you*
> *and have approved for you Islam as religion"*
> *(Prophet Muhammad s.a.w.)*

The 9th day of Thul-Hijjah is the day of Wu'Qoof. It is the most important day for the pilgrim. On this day the pilgrim must be present on Mount Arafat between Zawaal (midday) and the time of the Morning Prayer the following day. On this day of Arafat the pilgrims are the guests of Allah. Allah's mercy is said to be infinite and His generosity without boundaries. It is narrated that on this day Allah says to His angels, "My servants came to me through deep and distant mountain ways, matted and disheveled, craving and yearning for my Heaven, for even though your sins were so much as the number of grains of the sand or the drops of the rain or the foam of the sea, I will forgive you, you my servant may return with your sins being forgiven and for those on whose behalf you interceded."

Shireen and I were standing in line to board one of the thousands of diesel buses earmarked to take us to the plains of Mount Arafat. There was no pushing and shoving on this day. People were orderly and respectful. They might have pushed and shoved for a MacDonald's burger last night but today they were on their best behaviour. To have four million pilgrims all focused on a single goal, moving towards a single destination, is a sight that words cannot do justice to. You had to be there to experience the soldiery of the God. Very few police officers were in sight. Very little officialdom to marshal the troops was around. All these pilgrims had been schooled in their respective countries for this the most important day in the life of the Muslim pilgrim.

We boarded the bus, not the rust bucket on which we had arrived on in Medina, but a comfortable coach. However, air conditioning was missing. I reminded myself that we humans are never satisfied and decided not to sweat the small stuff. Within a few minutes we were en route to the plains of Arafat. Yes, all three hundred or so thousand buses with their diesel smoke bellowing its profanity into Allah's heavens. Again I decided to accept the environmental insult of my mode of transport. We were bumper to bumper with the other thousands of buses travelling at most 10km per hour. Occasionally people would disembark from the bus, while in motion, to use the occasional washroom facilities along the way. On this day the temperature exceeded 45 degree celsius with a level of humidity unmatched in the world. There was no water on the bus. And in order to help the pilgrims with their hydration needs, people were hurling packs of bottled water through open windows of the passing buses. I decided to hang my torso out of an open window in order to grip a 24 pack of cold water that a passerby was able to hand to me. The kindness of the people on this day was only trumped by the lack of organization by the Saudi organizers of the Hajj. Shireen reminded me that on this day I needed to be on my best behaviour which included keeping my emotions and my little demons in check. Every so often she would nudge me in the side as a reminder of the promise

I had made to her that this would indeed be my behaviour for the day. I had mentioned to you before that I was more careful of Shireen's wrath. Of course, today was special; I had to be cognizant of both Shireen's wrath and the mercy of Allah.

We crossed a bridge overlooking an ocean of people walking in the direction of Mount Arafat. Yes, millions of people all dressed in white robes walked slowly in the direction of Arafat. The heat was obviously not a problem for these committed souls. It looked like a river of people flowing from under the bridge. It was one of those indelible sights of Hajj for me. I reminded myself that one of the little demons in my mind, Marx, had once whispered, religions are "real" even though they serves as pacifying agents. This sight was real. I thanked Allah for giving me the pleasure of watching His soldiers march by. I brought salutations on His general Muhammad in appreciation of this physical vision.

A Hajj agent whom I had known for many years once mentioned to me that the official figures given for any Hajj were significantly less than the actual number as the Saudi royalty offer hundreds of thousands of visas unofficially for their personal bank accounts. He had personally sold these visas, by the thousands, in Indonesia, Malaysia, and a few other countries in the world. South Africa he said was one of a few countries where these types of "unofficial" visa sales were not engaged in. His reason for South Africa's exclusion from this activity lay purely in the pariah nature of the Muslim population. The Royals went after the big fish like Indonesia were his exact words. How true this story is I cannot say. Officially we were four million Gujaj. In reality it felt as if the entire world had descended on Makkah.

When we eventually arrived on Mount Arafat our South African designated camp had already been prepared. There were many large tents that we could occupy for the holy day. On this day Shireen reminded me we had to mind our p's and q's, read the Qur'an as often as possible, seek forgiveness for ourselves and family, we should pray in jama'a (group), we should recite the Salawaat (peace and grace) on the Prophet of Islam as often as possible, refrain from unlawful actions in word and deed. In fact, no unnecessary words should be uttered, and further, we were to engage in Thik'r (sacred religious utterances). She also reminded me that it was good to maintain the ritual ablution throughout the period on Arafat. I decided to follow her advice since on this day it was more about faith than knowledge. Besides, I was not going to dispute the oath taken by Allah that all was going to be forgiven on this auspicious day. I had learnt at an early age that science has not been able to replace religion. I had learnt at an early age that humans need religion exactly because science, unlike religion, cannot offer totalistic and ultimately unconfirmable responses to existential questions. All was going to be forgiven today. Science could not prove or disprove the forgiveness offered on Arafat that day. I opted for religion.

We made our prayers and we continued to mind our p's and q's. It felt good. There were people from various parts of South Africa present on that day. It was easy to see who stayed focused on Shireen's fatwas. Not all of us enjoy the equanimity of peace.

After a few hours there were many who could no longer sustain the discipline of focus. The Capetonians in our tent were either out to show how focused they could be or were truly in various states of contemplation. I remembered I was not allowed to judge and decided to erase unlawful thoughts from my mind. I witnessed many crying out of remorse. I witnessed many crying out of happiness. Some mentioned to me that it was as if their entire lives were replayed in their minds as if watching a movie. I did not cry. I felt no remorse. However, I felt as if all my burdens had been lifted. Shireen was crying. I did not enquire about feelings of remorse. I decided that it was between her and the God.

It was not my intention to listen in on a conversation between two elderly gentlemen from the Northern Province of South Africa in the tent next door. However, given their proximity I had no choice. One of the two started speaking at length. O People, lend me an attentive ear, for I know not whether after this year, I shall ever be amongst you again. Therefore listen to what I am saying to you very carefully and take these words to those who could not be present today.

O People, just as you regard this month, this day, this city as sacred, so regard the life and property of every Muslim as a sacred trust. Return the goods entrusted to you to their rightful owners. Hurt no-one, so that no-one may hurt you. Remember that you will indeed meet your Lord, and that He will indeed reckon your deeds. Allah has forbidden you to take usury, therefore all interest obligation shall henceforth be waived. Your capital, however, is yours to keep. You will neither inflict nor suffer any inequity.

Allah has judged that there shall be no interest and that all the interest due to 'Abbas ibn 'Abd al-Muttalib [Muhammad's uncle] shall henceforth be waived…

Beware Satan, for the safety of your religion. He has lost all hope that he will ever be able to lead you astray in big things, so beware of following him in small things.

O People, it is true that you have certain rights with regard to your women, but they also have rights over you. Remember that you have taken them as your wives only under Allah's trust and with His permission. If they abide by your right then to them belongs the right to be fed and clothed in kindness. Do treat your women well and be kind to them for they are your partners and committed helpers. And it is your right that they do not make friends with any one of whom you do not approve, as well as never to be unchaste.

O People, listen to me in earnest, worship Allah, say your five daily prayers, fast during the month of Ramadan, and give your wealth in zakat. Perform Hajj if you can afford to.

All mankind is from Adam and Hawwa, an Arab has no superiority over a non-Arab nor has a non-Arab any superiority over an Arab; also a white has no superiority over black nor a black any superiority over white except by piety and good action. Learn that every Muslim is a brother to every Muslim and that the Muslims constitute one brotherhood. Nothing shall be legitimate to a Muslim which belongs to a fellow Muslim unless it was given freely and willingly. Do not, therefore, do injustice to yourselves.

Remember, one day you will appear before Allah and answer your deeds. So beware, do not stray from the path of righteousness after I am gone.

O People, no prophet or apostle will come after me and no new faith will be born. Reason well, therefore, O People, and understand words which I convey to you. I leave behind me two things, the Qur'an and my example, the Sunna, and if you follow these you will never go astray.

All those who listen to me shall pass on my words to others and those to others again; and may the last ones understand my words better than those who listen to me directly. Be my witness, O Allah, that I have conveyed your message to your people.

I realized that he had read the Prophet's Last Sermon on Mount Arafat. How appropriate, I thought. This was the most famous message delivered on this calendar day, in this very geography, by the most influential person in the history of Islam, or perhaps for that matter, the most influential individual in the history of humankind. I thought through some of what was said. The focus was on "right conduct" toward the property of others. The care for human feelings – hurt no one – compassion. "Right action" in the Islamic context toward capital – no interest – is insisted on. The Devil is involved in minor disturbances. Humans ultimately triumph over the big issues in religion. There exists a reciprocal relationship between men and women. Be kind to your female partners and they should remain loyal to their male partners. The five pillars of Islam should be upheld. There is no one ethnic group to be superior over another. Egalitarianism in race relations is insisted on. We will all ultimately be answerable to the God. Islam will be the last of the major world traditions. The Qur'an and the Prophet's example are to be the guidelines for Islam. But most striking was the Prophet's last wish: to have those furthest removed in history, in other words those Muslims in the present, understand his message even clearer than the saghabah (disciples) present at the last sermon.

I wanted the people back home to hear this message. They were discriminating against people of colour. They were so often accused of taking the material of fellow brothers. They cared little for the feelings of others. They were party to interest in their capitalist countries. They often treated their women with disrespect. I was convinced that most did not pay the zakat. Those of Indian descent held other Muslims in contempt. But most importantly, they insisted that our dead forefathers understood the Prophet's message better than those living in their midst. How sad I thought, the Prophet's wish was still to be realized.

Time on Arafat had passed faster than I had anticipated. It was dark and our busses were waiting to transport us to Muzdalifah. Shireen and I were happy to be seated in the diesel combustor anxiously awaiting the next installment of rituals. It was easy; we had both surrendered to Allah. We were instruments in religious motion. Not even death scared us now. We were cleansed of sin.

If ever I welcomed death, this was the moment in time. All was forgiven. We were above the angels at this point. We were vassals of purity. On that day we were baked clay carrying only the spirit of Allah in our bodies. There was nothing profane here, only the sacred. My little demons were silent, even those German viruses. Maybe they were outlawed on Arafat, I thought.

Chapter 13: Al-Mash'aril-Haraam

> *"Rab'ba'naa aa 'tinaa fid'dun'yaa ha'sa'na'taw wa'fil aa'khi'rati ha'sa'na'taw wa'qi'naa a'thaa'ban naar"*
> *[Our Lord! Give us good in this world and good in the hereafter, and protect us from the torment of the fire]*

It was sunset when we left Arafat for Muzdalifah. Shireen reminded me that as pilgrims we should maintain our state of humbleness and piety. I reminded myself that we were all actors on a stage and that the occasion demanded a religious demeanour and deference. She continued her fatwa. Remember that we should continue our Thik'r, she insisted. She also reminded me that this night was the eve of Eidul-Ad'Haa (one of the two festive days on the Muslim calendar). It was necessary for the pilgrim to be present at Muzdalifah after the second half of the night and remain there until sun rise if possible, the Sheikha continued. Shireen also reminded me to collect my seven pebbles here. We were to use these pebbles to pelt the Jamarah (heap of stones or Satan as the little traditionalists of the faith would have it). I was not going to contest her fatwas as I was convinced that science had not yet offered rational explanations for most of the existential questions in my mind. I was looking forward to pelting those demons. The pebbles were to be the size of a pea. I was tempted to include a few larger stones for those German demons in my head but decided to stay with convention.

We arrived at Muzdalifah. It was no more than flat desert lands. The Saudi government was certainly not concerned about the washroom facilities here. There must have been, at most, five blocks of toilets for four million pilgrims. I stood in a line-up of about one hundred thousand pilgrims to use the loo. In the end I had to find a private bush as I would have had to wait fifteen days to relieve myself. It is great to own a monopoly. It is even better when that monopoly is guaranteed by religion, the little demon whispered. I was intent on keeping her quiet but this night she overpowered me momentarily.

Our bus was to leave within an hour. We had to find our pelting ammunition in the darkness of Muzdalifah. I wondered if there were stones left after fourteen centuries of pebble-hunting. For a while there the thought crossed my mind that the Saudis had to truck in loads of pebbles for the occasion. However, the scarcity of these stones on the occasion quickly dispelled the idea. Once we were on the bus I noticed the care with which our fellow pilgrims guarded their stones. A few older people were asking around for a few extra pebbles as the darkness obviously had an impact on their geological excavations. I had mined a few extra nuggets and gladly handed these around. Maybe one of my stones would strike the Big Satan. Maybe I will be rewarded for being so forward-thinking. I quickly stopped this line of blasphemy. I reminded myself of the message passed to me by the blind Sufi not so long ago,"You are a nothing, don't think you are special, you are only the instrument of Allah". This put stop to my ego almost immediately.

Across from us sat a couple from Bosnia. I was curious to find out more about the Bosnian genocide. I wanted to know more than the images and messages that CNN wanted us to believe. It turned out that the husband was a medical specialist in the city of Sarajevo. We had an hour to wait before our nitrous- carbon- producer would move. The driver did not even care to turn off the engine for the hour. I was told fuel is cheaper than water here. Amidst the noise of the diesel engine I engaged my learned friend.

Vladimir and Katja was a couple in their early forties. They raised a young boy and girl during the trying years between April 1992 and February 1996 in Sarajevo. One could tell by their facial expressions that it was years of pain that they were happy to have left behind. Vladimir did most of the talking. From the very beginning, it was a matter of unhappiness by the Yugoslav nationalist agents as the Republic of Bosnia Herzegovina had opted for independence. There were territories in this new independent state that the Yugoslavians had aspirations to. Already in March of 1992 the Yugoslav army had set up sniper positions around the city of Sarajevo. The citizens came out in protest against this potential conflict through marches around the city while the snipers had their sights firmly set and ready to pull their triggers. Sporadic fighting had also already begun between the Yugoslavian army and the Bosnian Herzegovina army.

Every morning when Vladimir and Katja walked to the hospital, where Vladimir held a position as head of the Intensive Care Unit, they were forced to walk two hundred meters apart in the event that a bomb was dropped or a mortar shell was fired in their direction. Vladimir explained that they could not afford to be killed at the same time as they had to think about the future care of their young children. The food shortage during the years of war was so severe that Vladimir dropped thirty kilograms over a period of two months. They would cook the small rations of rice that they could lay their hands on to feed the children first then drink the rice water as a tea substitute. Vladimir was smart enough to think about the nutrition of his growing young children and as he says, he did not want his children's development to be affected over the long-term. The sacrifices that a parent would go through for their children are acts of compassion unmatched, I thought.

Vladimir explained that he was the proud owner of a set of encyclopaedia. These voluminous texts he used to cover the windows of his father-in-law's apartment in order to keep out sniper fire. Sadly it was not enough. His father-in-law was the victim of a sharp-shooter who was able to penetrate the weakest point in the window covering. Katja could not attend the funeral as the risk was too high to have both of them at the funeral in case again of bombings where both might have been killed. It was also not that easy to find gas to transport the dead body to the cemetery. Fortunately Vladimir was able to negotiate two litres of gas to lay the father-in-law to rest.

Of all the Yugoslavian tactics, the sniper fire was by far the most nerve wracking, continued Vladimir. He once had a young patient, Jamil, who frequented the hospital with a chronic ailment. The twenty-two year old Jamil would visit his clinic three times a week. On one of these visitations the nurses reported to Vladimir that Jamil was sitting on the steps of the hospital staring out at the heavens. Vladimir was concerned that Jamil would be shot by sniper fire and quickly made his way to the entrance of the hospital in order to escort his favourite patient indoors. He called to Jamil to rather sit indoors but received no response from the young man. Instinctively Vladimir moved towards Jamil in order to grab his attention and to help the young man inside. Vladimir was of course putting his own life at risk by going outside facing the sharp shooters hidden on the hills surrounding Sarajevo. Gently Vladimir tapped Jamil on the head to grab his intention. When Vladimir retrieved his hand, he had a part of Jamil's brain stuck onto his fingers. The snipers had killed Jamil during the five minutes that the young man had sat down to enjoy a few puffs of his rolled tobacco before entering the hospital. Tears started rolling down Vladimir's cheeks as he continued.

I was listening intently. Shireen tried to engage Katja on another topic while Vladimir poured his heart out to me. The United Nations, the superpowers including the United States were aware of our plight but did nothing. It seemed they were playing a waiting game. We felt they were deliberately delaying intervention because we were only Muslims. We felt our lives were valued less. We were determined to fight for our less equitable lives. We turned to Allah for help. It seemed as if Allah was slow in response. Why did we have to lose our innocent children and family? Why did Allah allow this to happen to us? Why did Allah allow innocent children and women to be raped? We questioned the mercy of Allah. We wanted to know where Allah was in all of this. We rationalized that Allah knows best. We rationalized that we do not know the workings of Allah. The Bosnian Sheikhs argued that it was the will of Allah. It did not make sense to me, Vladimir continued. I came on Hajj to ask Allah to give me answers to all my questions that could not be answered by religion and my Sheikhs. I had to know how Allah could allow so many innocent children to die so very violently after having done nothing to incur such terror. I am yet to get a response from Allah. However, there are still a few days left on the journey. I am told Allah is most merciful. I so much want to believe this, Vladimir continued.

I had no response for my new brother in Islam. I had learnt at an early age that religions cannot answer these difficult questions. I had asked myself many related questions over and over again whilst travelling through the God's forsaken continent, Africa. I pondered: Why would the God kill off millions of innocent children who had contracted HIV/AIDS? Why would the God keep black South Africa in poverty after hundreds of years of oppression and the most evil forms of discrimination known to humankind? What did these innocent children do to die of hunger at so young an age while the developed world dumps its excess food productions? Where is the fairness in the God's rationale? I had to remind myself that I was taught at an early age not to question the God. Today I was furious and struggled to keep my emotions in check. I looked at Vladimir and realized that here was someone who had lost more than I did. In my life in South Africa I had only lost my dignity and self-respect due to apartheid. At least I was able to now rebuild it. Vladimir had lost relatives and friends. Vladimir had lost his trust in the God.

My friend continued. We now live in Canada. We were fortunate to escape with a few suitcases and were offered refuge in Canada provided I never again practice medicine in my new country. They only trust their own system. When I watch their doctors at work I sometimes long to work in my old profession but respect the undertaking I had agreed to. My family's freedom and safety was worth more than my personal career. The sacrifices that a parent would go through for their children are acts of the highest compassion I reminded myself once more. Vladimir was a God in this respect. Or rather, it was the spirit of the God in him that constantly surfaced.

We completed our morning prayer outside the bus in congregation with our new acquaintances, Vladimir and Katja. I asked Vladimir to lead the prayer. I afforded him the respect of leader given his qualifications as an uncompromising parent. I was certain the God would recognise his own spirit. I shed a tear after the prayer as Vladimir asked the God to forgive his dead relatives who died so young. I cried as Vladimir asked Allah to forgive the Yugoslavians who had raped his relatives and killed Jamil. I could tell that Vladimir was honest in asking forgiveness for his family's murderers. It was as if Vladimir's body was only a vassal carrying the purity of Allah's ruh (spirit). I felt I was in the company of the God. I reminded myself, that we had just left Arafat. Vladimir's essence was pure spirit of the God. He was sinless, I was sinless, Shireen was sinless, and Katja was sinless. We were spirits of the God in prayer that moment. There could be no purer congregation in the Muslim world than that moment after Arafat on Muzdalifah. The clergy back home will attest to this.

Chapter 14: Mina and the Visions of 911

> *"The teachings of Islam can fail under no circumstances.*
> *With all our systems of culture and civilization,*
> *we cannot go beyond Islam and, as a matter of fact,*
> *no human mind can go beyond the Koran."*
> Johann Goethe, cited in Sir Henry Elliot's Letters of Johann Goethe, 1865.

We left Muzdalifah after the Morning Prayer. Shireen started her fatwas again. We were to remain in piety, remain humble and modest and continue with our religious utterances. I was excited. We would pelt the Jamaratul-Aqabah (big Satan) this day.

Mina was a makeshift tent city. The Saudi officials had prepared tents for all groups of pilgrims. There were no hotels here, just tents. Grand tents with air-conditioning were arranged for the pilgrims from North America and Europe. Not-so-grand tents for those pilgrims from Africa. When we arrived at our tent it was occupied by a group from Cape Town. We did not have the energy to argue or negotiate with the occupants and decided instead to squat outside our designated tent. Shireen reminded me that it was better to control our emotions on this day. We were to stay focused on the rituals ahead and avoid any confrontation as the three major Satans were in the area awaiting their stoning. A fellow pilgrim remarked that the devil was loose in this part of the world and did everything in her power to distract the pilgrim from the rituals ahead. Four million pilgrims from all parts of the world had come to pelt these demons; I was not going to argue with the learned pilgrim.

We slept under the dark skies that night. At least a trillion stars were evident. I thought about the life of the prophet of Islam contemplating the revealed messages at night in the desert of seventh century Arabia. Thousands of square kilometers of sand surrounded him, with the lights of the stars his only navigational points. No wonder the moon and the star became the totem for Islam, I thought. These must have been the only lights of hope during those long contemplative nights. I was jealous at the thought of those early desert-dwellers who enjoyed the peace and tranquility of the desert surrounds. They had all the time in the world to think things through. It was all about tranquility and peace after a long day in battle for those Bedouin of Islam.

Peace, yes Islam literally means Peace. At least this is how I interpreted the consonance in the word Islam. Many of my friends were not aware of the fact that the Arabic language has no vowels. It is only the Qur'an that has the vowels inserted. This is to allow non-Arab speakers to pronounce the Qur'anic text with a higher degree of accuracy. The word Islam could thus have a variety of meanings out of context, including peace, submission or surrender to mention but a few. In the desert with only your camels for company, under a contemplative sky, peace comes to mind, I thought.

Shireen and I found comfort that night under the Arabian sky. Shireen grouped together with some of the women in one corner while I lay flat on my back next to some Muslim brothers from different parts of the world. The brother on my left hand side was rather distant in his manner. He introduced himself as Muhammad. I had learned early in life that all humans need affirmation. I had learned early in life that all humans enjoy acknowledgment. I had learned early in life that humans thrive on endorsement. I affirmed, acknowledged and endorsed whatever little my neighbour Muhammad had to say. I respected his personal space that he covertly demanded. Resourcefully I moved my social style, in demeanor and deference, in line with his level of assertiveness and emotion. I wanted to hear him speak. I was told by the brother on my right that he was special. I was told by the brother on my right that he was a member of Al-Qaeda. I had never met such a warrior. I was hungry to hear his tales.

Muhammad was obviously educated. He had acquired his Islamic education in Pakistan and his engineering training in Germany. He had spent time doing military training in Afghanistan where he remained to help in the fight against the Russians. The Americans had funded their campaign against the Communists but withdrew their support when political conditions changed between the two superpowers, he said. Over time he became disillusioned with capitalism, secularism, and a win-lose orientation to all negotiations in life. Over time he became disillusioned with western hegemony. His worldview moved ever so slowly in favour of an Islamic way of life, Muhammad continued. My little demon quickly whispered,"What does an Islamic way of life mean"?"Is there only one Islamic way of life?" the little German demon insisted. I had to keep them in check, I may never have this opportunity again, I thought. Muhammad continued:"I had befriended a wealthy Saudi who leads us in jihad (holy war) against the West. We will soon show the enemy that Allah can favour the underdog in battle," Muhammad continued. Remember the Battle of Badr where three hundred Muslims were able to conquer an army many times more in number, he asked. The small Muslim army was triumphant against the infidels there, so will we be, he remarked confidently.

We have a sophisticated plan that will shake the world, he insisted. I continued to affirm, acknowledge and endorse my learned brother in order to hear his plan. I must admit, I was not at all strategic in my communication. It was an honest attempt with spontaneous responses to hear his master plan. Muhammad pointed out that it is easy to strike an unsuspecting opponent and that the element of surprise was on their side. I quickly enquired if he supported suicide bombing. His response was immediate,"Only if it is carefully orchestrated and the casualties on the enemy side were significant are you on the right path," brother Muhammad insisted. Only this suicide attack will make Pearl Harbour wane in comparison to what we have in mind he told me. I could sense a nervousness and excitement in his manner that were previously absent.

We will enter the United States of America as citizen at a specified airport then board different planes to different cities. After take-off we will wrestle control of the planes and re-route the journey to high-density locations where we will then fly these jumbos into skyscrapers. We will cause devastation of unprecedented enormity, Muhammad continued. At this juncture I had had enough of my neighbour's wishful thinking and decided to excuse myself from his company. For a moment I thought that my little demons had escaped and had found new form in the shape of my neighbours Muhammad and Ata. After all, I thought, this is the station where they were supposed to disembark. They were to be pelted by the millions of pilgrim. These gentlemen were certainly not of sound mind and especially on such a sacred occasion where hatred and blasphemy was supposedly forbidden. I had to find another place of rest. Shireen and I left the site with the excuse that a fellow countryman had offered us shelter from the cold in another tent. I was happy not to reveal the encounter to Shireen. I was careful of her wrath. I decided to forget about the demons in Muhammad's mind. At least mine were not violent. For the first time I felt at peace with the sarcasm and wit of my monsters.

Unfortunately we were not able to find new sleeping spots under tent. Again we lay under the watchful eyes of the moon and the stars, albeit a few hundred meters away from our violent friends. For a while there I thought about Sheikh Vaybier's "warrior rather than a scholar" painting of the ideal typical Muslim. Here was a scholar turned warrior. Is the warrior in us so strong that attempts at scholarly ways can only be temporary? I wondered what Sheikh Vaybier's ancestor would say about this. At this point I was happy to be watching the beggars in the street rather than listen to the scholar-warrior further down the street from us.

The following morning we watched the warriors of Allah march by, nation by nation, en route to pelt the Jamarah. Our South African delegation along with a few other African nations had our turn in the afternoon. There were hundreds of thousands of pilgrims frantically pelting away ahead of us. I was certain that the elderly amongst us would never be able to come within striking distance of the demons. A few of the stronger warriors in our group decided to form a ring chained together by holding hands with the elderly protected inside. The idea was to escort the frail as close as possible to the pelting stations so that they could fulfill their ritual of stoning. We marshaled our way through the crowds through brute force with the elderly marching comfortably inside the ring. Once we had achieved success we decided to continue this innovation for the rest of the elderly who were not accommodated the first time around. Some of the elderly were so afraid that they shivered and cried. They were convinced that they had to complete this ritual. They were aware that many of their loved ones had died in the past in their attempts to stone the Jamarah. Some of them remembered that they had lost relatives through this stampede. I remembered my aunt Ghadija and uncle Manie who were left for dead here. I pelted with vigour when the sight of my lost relatives appeared that moment. I was hoping my little demons would voice their opinions. They remained silent throughout the ritual.

We left the pelting station satisfied. I had lost one of my sandals. As I hobbled away from "the heap of stones" I passed a mountain of sandals that were piled on one side of Jamarah Aqabah (Big Satan). Mine must be amongst those I thought. It felt good to have left something behind in battle. Shireen reminded me that the men would now have to have their heads shaved. My little demon surfaced, you will not only have lost your sandal, he whispered.

We were exhausted when we returned to Makkah. The circumambulation and the ritual of the Sai had to be done before we could retire. It was difficult to stay focused in a state of tiredness. I had learnt early in my life that humans need sleep. I had learnt early in life that the body would be able to continue with physical activity continuously for six months if the brain was disconnected from the body. I had learnt early that it is the brain that needs restoration. I had learnt early that Allah boasts that all his creatures need sleep. I had learnt early in life that only Allah is independent of sleep. I slept knowing that the Hajj was complete.

Chapter 15: Farewell to the Sacred

"Alhamdulillah hirabil alamin"
[All praises to The God, the god (or lord) of the (entire) world]

We were ready to leave Makkah. For the first time in our journey Shireen started yearning for Shameer. I had to constantly remind her that we were leaving the following day. All that was left was the farewell circumambulation and the farewell Sai. My mind was focused on making as many revolutions around the Kabah as possible for the remaining time as I worked from the vantage point that I would possibly never return to this sacred place of Abraham and Muhammad.

An unexpected sadness came over me. It was as if my soul was at once happy and sad. Shireen had other things to do, including the final purchasing of gifts for our expectant well-wishers back home. She had also still to purchase her modering (costume to disembark with on arrival). The modering ritual is an old Cape Townian custom that Shireen had heard of by the numerous Gujaj that she had met over the period of our visitation. That said, Shireen was naturally predisposed to haute couture. I had told you before how she loved shopping. Well, shopping for beautiful clothes was her first love. The modering ritual became a fard (obligatory).

We spent many hours walking the steep hills of Makkah to find the best dressmaker or shop to fit together all the components of Shireen's outfit. Wherever we visited, we found queues of Cape Townians with similar wants. I began to suspect that a competition existed between the Gujaj from this region of South Africa. The prize for the best dressed Gujaj was the admiration and envy of the well-wishers back home. I was convinced that Shireen would win this unspoken prize. I was not sure about the partner that accompanied her. I was never one for fashion. However, on this occasion Shireen insisted that she was not going to be seen with an "also ran". I always thought that my large unkempt beard would win the sacred admiration of the people in my surrounds. Shireen had other ideas for me.

Boeta Mustapha, a rather plain character, approached me about my thoughts about modering. I must say, I was caught by surprise when the old man giggled while boasting a rather large red Turkish hat that he found both amusing and handsome. The red hat had a long black tassel dangling along its side. I was quickly given the history of this sacred hat. It was the Ottoman Empire's export to Cape Town during the 1860s. When the black tassel is added to the hat it signifies that the person wearing this fancy headgear had been on Hajj. In other words, you were dealing with a Hajji. This was to be Boeta Mustapha's only accoutrement. I was convinced that Shireen would be more than happy with this historical totem on her husband's head. I had learnt early in life that fashion was important. I had also learnt early in life that this was not enough as we humans often play covert conflict games.

The most common of the covert conflict games that Shireen and I would have to engage on arrival included, Yes but, now I've got you, you son of a gun, mine is worse than yours and blemish. I was convinced that when I arrive home with my red hat someone will remark, that the Hajji is sporting a beautiful hat to which someone in the group will respond: yes but, it does not fit well with the black cloak that he is wearing. I was also not certain whether Boeta Mustapha was setting me up. When I get back home with my fancy red hat, my large beard and fancy red hat may constitute a fashion faux pas, in this event Boeta Mustapha may respond, now I've got you, you son of a gun. If I ask a friend back home what he thought about my hat he may blemish it by responding, it is great-looking but what about the extra weight that you picked up on your journey. If I coyly tell a friend about all the trouble and effort I had to go through in acquiring this fashion item he might respond with "You had to see the immense trouble I went through in acquiring a hat when I returned from Hajj." I had learnt early in life that people operate largely through these games of covert conflict in communication. I decided to rather leave the Ottoman totem in Makkah. Shireen would have to find something suitable in its place. I was not qualified to make such an important decision.

The time had come to vacate our one-star motel. Our bags were packed. We left the room burdened with baggage and sadness. We left the room to perform our final ritual of the farewell circumambulation and the Sai.

Shireen and I decided to do these rituals together. We circled the Kabah side-by- side. Shireen was still reciting her Arabic verses. I remained with my Afrikaans. I now realised that most of the strangers passing us in this ritual were speaking in Urdu, Turkish or Indonesian. I was convinced the God understood all of us, even Shireen. In my prayers I asked the God for the forgiveness of my family and friends. I asked the God for the forward prosperity and wealth of my family and friends. I asked the God to guide my sister Rehana in her quest to bear a child. I asked the God to bring peace in the future marriage of my brother Gilman. I asked the God to calm Shireen's wrath. I forgot to ask the God for a gift for myself. The thought never crossed my mind. Only when the ritual was completed did my little demon intercede with,"You humans need gifts from the God in this world and in the world hereafter." This time I agreed with the little monster.

We made our way to the Sai. This would be the last time that I would have to walk that grating pebble walkway. I was happy that my feet would not have to endure the pain of this journey again. I was sad that I would say goodbyes to the trials of Hagar. When I finally reached the destination of Mount Marwa, I stood alone looking down onto the Kabah. It lay before me in its splendour. I was stunned for a moment at the magnificence of this sight. I was awe-inspired by the power that these stones below me had exercised on the billions of Muslims of the past. Then, uninvited, the blind Sufi appeared. His voice piercing yet comforting,"Ask Allah for any thing in life that you wish for"."Remember," he continued, "you are only a human. You need the God's gifts in this life and the year after." How opposing to my little demon Karl Marx, I thought. This Muslim was insisting that religion offer salvation both in this life and in the life hereafter. This was not to be opium to lull the indignities of this life, but opium to enjoy both here and the eschaton. I must be honest, I struggled with a request for a gift. I thought about asking for ten million

US dollars but decided against this as I knew that I would soon spend it. I thought about asking for four wives but realised that I could not even handle the wrath of Shireen. I thought about asking to be the political leader of the United States of America but realised that I would then have to at sometime compromise my ethics and at another time use violence to impose my will. Time was running out. Finally I had it. I humbly asked the God to lead me on a path of knowledge and the attainment of inner peace. I was shy when I asked this. I was not always the brightest and the most peaceful among my friends. However, I had learnt early in life that money and peace do not always find synergy. I had learnt early that women and eroticism find a position at the opposite spectrum of rationality. I had learnt early that the politician has often to compromise her integrity. I had learnt early in life that the most difficult task in life is to know who you truly are. I opted for gnosis through knowledge and peace. I opted for Islam.

Shireen and I made our way to the airport. I excused myself to use the washroom facilities. Shireen was dressed in her modering; I had still to decide on mine. In front of a small mirror in the washroom I carefully removed my beard. I found my favourite jeans that always travelled with me and donned this fashion icon along with an ordinary white shirt and a pair of well-worn sneakers. I decided to add the only fashion garb that would link me to the Hajj: a very ordinary looking fez (religious hat). Shireen did not recognize me at first. Boeta Mustapha walked passed me at least thrice before I had to pull him by the sleeve of his shirt to remind him that his friend Kimal was seeking his attention.

Both Shireen and Boeta Mustapha were stunned at the sight of the profanity of all of this. I offered no explanation.

I left my demons in that washroom. I left my ego in that washroom. I decided that the greatest Muslims are those ordinary people who ask no questions. I decided that the best of those on the Hajj are those who are not plagued by the millions of critical questions by little monsters. I decided that the best are those who do not question the use of language and continue on in tongues. I decided to join the party of the ordinary. I reminded myself,"You are a nothing, don't think you are special, you are only the instrument of Allah". I reminded myself that this was my first lesson towards knowledge and peace.

The Kiswah is the black cloth that covers the Kabah